THE QUANTUM GHOST

JONATHAN BALLAGH

THE QUANTUM GHOST
Copyright © 2017 by Jonathan Ballagh
ISBN: 978-0-9967138-5-6 (print)
ISBN: 978-0-9967138-4-9 (ebook)
All Rights Reserved.

Edited by David Gatewood
www.lonetrout.com

Formatting by Knite and Day Design
www.kniteandday.com

Cover design and interior illustrations by Ben J. Adams
www.benjadams.com

for Mom & Dad

PROLOGUE

THE DYING LIGHT flared crimson and orange, sinking under the weight of the evening sky until at last it vanished. A breeze came with nightfall, chilling the air and twisting the leaves of the old willow that grew from the grass and stones at the water's edge. Its branches swayed like delicate strands of hair, autumn gold, and just beneath them, shadows crept over the pond.

A speck of light appeared over the water, then quickly lengthened into a blinding vertical sliver. When it touched the surface of the pond, the earth moved with a thunderous boom, shaking loose a flock of birds from the tree. The light grew sideways now, expanding into a rippling torch, broader than the willow and just as tall. The water shimmered blue from the electric vapors floating above it.

The door had opened, and it burned like an icy flame, steady and cold in the quiet air.

Suddenly, a ghostly form fell backward through the light—a mechanical figure, white plastic wrapping a skeleton of steel. A ribbon of smoke curled from its scorched abdomen, and for a moment, the robot appeared to hang in the air.

The illusion was shattered when the door collapsed; time snapped back, and the bot splashed down. The pond sprayed and hissed, smoke mixing with steam. One of the bot's arms covered its billowing stomach; the other cradled a glowing dome.

As the bot sank beneath the water, it held the radiant dome above the surface. When even its fingertips were submerged, the dome still remained afloat, bobbing lazily in the eerie quiet.

Waiting.

PART 1

CHAPTER 1

MIND OVER MATTER

Sometime in the near future...

FROM ANOTHER WORLD, she heard the dog's distant whine. Faint, but with unmistakable desperation. She heard it above the rumbles, the explosions, the whizzing, the clashing of swords—the sounds of battle. She heard it—and then did her best to forget about it.

Her thumbs bounced across the tablet, passing through holographic warriors that marched to unspeakable doom. The last fight had weakened her ranks; still she pushed forward, further than she had ever gone and more determined than ever. A castle grew from the screen, dirt churning as it erupted from the earth. The enemy's troops spewed from the stronghold; villainous, angry, and frothing mad, they approached her soldiers.

Her eyes narrowed.

Another whine sounded from downstairs.

Hold on, she thought. *Almost there...*

The whining persisted, more urgent than before, and then—

"Can you please let Duke out?" her mother called from the kitchen.

Somewhere deep in her mind, Remi registered the request, but she never wavered from the game. She couldn't afford to—not when she was this close, when she could taste the victory that was only minutes away. One slip, and it was over. And besides, the dog was her brother's responsibility, not hers.

Let him deal with it.

She regained her focus and steadied her grip, and her score continued to climb. She loved this game. These days, it was her favorite way to pass the time.

"Take the dog out, Remi Cobb! I know you're up there. Give that game a rest, would you?"

And that was all it took. Her concentration was broken… and her game was over. Her soldiers waved their weapons angrily and unleashed a furious cry before collapsing into pixelated dust that blew to the edges of the screen and dissolved.

"Where's James?" Remi hollered.

"Your brother and sister are out with your father," her mom called back. "And I'm busy making sure your dinner doesn't catch fire! So I'm not going to ask again!"

Remi flung her tablet onto the comforter, leapt off the bed, and huffed down the stairs, anger swelling with each step. *Stupid James*, she thought. Getting a dog was all his idea—not that she'd put up much of a fight—and he'd promised to take care of it. An empty promise *that* had proven to be.

She found Duke in the mudroom, waiting impatiently by the back door, his nails clicking eagerly on the linoleum floor. Smells of rolls and beef stew wafted in from the kitchen. Dinner would be ready soon, and she wanted to get this over with as quickly as possible.

No sooner had she cracked the outside door than Duke forced it the rest of the way open and rocketed past her into the night, nearly bowling her over in the process. Muttering under her breath, Remi stepped to the edge of the deck and leaned against the railing, watching the dog's shadow disappear down the hill that led from her house to the pond. The autumn air ran through her short red hair and felt cold against her skin. She wrapped herself in her arms and shivered, dreading the winter that meant even more time at home, more time inside. As if that were even possible.

After a couple of minutes, her mind wandered back to the warmth of the kitchen, where the food had to be waiting by now.

"Come on, Duke! Let's go!"

She heard a far-off whimper, then silence. The lab didn't return, but then again, he seldom did—a fact she'd pointed out to her brother on more than one occasion. James said it was just part of his charm, that he had trained his dog to ignore her.

She looked back at the kitchen window and saw her mom shifting about inside. *Busy as always*, Remi thought, feeling sorry for her mom. She decided she wouldn't bother her with this; she would take care of Duke herself. But where was he?

She gazed over the rail. Beyond the pond, the land sloped down again, giving way to the orchard trees that darkened the horizon like fallen black clouds. Maybe he had wandered under them.

"Come on, boy—now!" she shouted as loud as she could.

Still nothing. She felt a nagging worry building in her, but she dismissed it and headed for the deck stairs. She had just reached the grass when, in the distance, Duke began barking, frantic and wild, with a sharp, fearful edge—almost a yelp. The hairs on her neck stood up—he had never sounded like that before.

Remi bounded down the hill toward the pond. Following the barks, she found the lab standing at the edge of the water, his tail up and teeth bared.

"Duke?" she whispered, creeping forward.

The dog ignored her, continuing his watch. At least he had stopped barking.

She inched closer to the water, growing more timid with each step. Wisps of mist drifted up from its surface. The crisp air smelled of mowed grass and something else—something acrid, toxic. Then she saw something floating on the water: an eerie light behind fingers of curling fog. She squinted to get a better look. It was a glowing dome, with rings of sequined light that grew and retreated around it.

Remi stepped over to the dog and put her trembling hand out to ease him. "What do you think it is?" she asked, crouching down.

Duke kept his eyes on the water and responded with a soft growl.

The light pulsed in a slow, hypnotic rhythm.

Her world felt very small now, very still.

She couldn't look away.

Suddenly, a hand splashed through the surface—pale white, with long, skeletal fingers. They fell across the dome, gripping it tightly, and pulled it under.

Remi covered her mouth with both hands to stifle her scream. The water rippled, then went still. Whatever had been there was gone. The mist had already returned to fill in the gap.

She rubbed her eyes and turned toward Duke. At first, she was too scared to speak, then her courage returned. "Please tell me you saw that."

The dog gazed up at her, panting softly as though nothing had happened.

She wondered if anything really had.

XOXOX

Remi found her father waiting back at the house, arms crossed over his sweater, propping the door open with his foot. He frowned into his beard, and the worry shone in his tired eyes. "Everything okay?" he asked, reaching down to pat the dog as he brushed by.

"I'm okay, Dad. There was—" Seeing that familiar look on her father's face, she said, "For once, please stop worrying."

He sighed, started to say something, but then appeared to think better of it. Wrinkling his nose and adjusting his glasses, he stepped aside to let her pass.

Inside she found the table already set, dinner served, and her family waiting for her. The table had bench seating, and Liv, Remi's younger sister, sat next to James on one side, while their mother sat alone on the other.

"Let's get to it, then," her father said, carrying the last of the food over and squeezing his large frame in next to his wife. He cracked his knuckles and set to work ladling steaming bowls of soup for his family.

"Get lost out there?" James joked, following it up with an obnoxious slurp.

She glared at him as she slid in beside her father, keeping as far from her brother as she could manage.

"What?" James whined.

"You *know* what," Remi fired back. "Next time, walk your own dog." She tore off a hunk of roll, dipped it into her soup, and chewed furiously.

"So sorry," James said, insincerely. "Liv and I were at the store with Dad. You know—doing our best to help out—unlike *some* people around here."

Remi met his grin with a scowl. Across the table, Liv rolled her eyes and stuck out her tongue, motioning sideways at her brother with her thumb. James jabbed her in the side with an elbow. An argument broke out seconds later.

Remi forced a smile and continued the meal in silence, ignoring the commotion. Her mind kept going back to the pond—and the *thing* she had seen there.

Before she knew it, she was alone at the table, the dishes cleared except for her own. She was left twirling her spoon over a half-empty bowl.

Only James was still in the kitchen with her; he had been tasked with doing the dishes tonight. "Hurry up and finish. I've got other things to do," he said, annoyed.

She rolled her eyes and debated whether to tell him what had happened. It would make her sound weird, but then again, her brother already thought she was crazy. She figured she had nothing to lose.

"Um, hey, James… I need to tell you something."

She looked sheepishly up at her big brother. He was way taller, tall like her dad was; thin, with short spiky hair and heavy rimmed glasses that turned his eyes into two huge rectangles. Her mom said they gave him an "air of sophistication," but she knew better.

James stopped the water and dried his hands. "Sure—what's up?"

"I know how stupid this sounds, but I saw something earlier. There's a… thing in our pond. Something…" She paused, feeling more embarrassed than she thought possible. "I don't know… I think it was an alien or something."

James arched an eyebrow and smiled, his glasses sliding down his nose. "Sure there is." He nudged the frames back up with a finger, turned the water back on, and resumed his chore.

"Jerk! I'm serious—I saw it earlier!" She wadded up her napkin and tossed it at him. "You know, when I was doing *your* job—taking care of Duke."

"What did this *alien* look like then?"

"I told you it would sound stupid."

"Well, it does."

"I didn't see all of it, just a—" She hesitated, feeling foolish. "—a hand. A ghost's hand… I think. Duke was barking at this glowing ball floating on the water, maybe the size of a football, and then this hand came out of the water and grabbed it. And there was this weird kind of smoke all around, something burning, and—"

James's laugh cut her off. "Wait! Did you say *ghost*? What's wrong with you, Remi? Better not let Mom and Dad find out."

"Yeah, believe me, I know how they are. Just… would you come down with me and make sure there's nothing there?"

"You're almost thirteen now," James said. "It's time to quit it with all these stories and grow up."

She could tell he immediately regretted his choice of words.

"Sorry, Remi. I know—"

"Maybe I have to make up my own stories because you're actually allowed to *do* stuff, James. You're not stuck here all day. Mom and Dad don't treat you like a prisoner."

Her brother's face softened. "You know they can't help it. They're doing the best they can. We all are."

"I know." She rapped her spoon on the table. "Look—just this once, please just come take a look with me when you're done."

He stared at her, drying a bowl with a dishcloth.

"Please?"

"Okay—fine!" James growled. "But only if you promise to never bother me again."

)(O)(O)(

The flashlight app on James's phone created a blinding beam that cut through the fog. He moved it around slowly, illuminating the surface of the pond.

There was nothing there.

He let the light linger on the water to prove his point, then glared at his sister.

"What?" Remi said. "I'm not lying! I swear I saw something."

"It's the mist—it's got you spooked. You're seeing things in it."

Remi closed her eyes, sighed, shook her head. She knew he wouldn't believe her. But then again, why would he? She wasn't even sure she trusted herself. And whatever she had seen was obviously long gone by now—if she had actually seen it in the first place.

"Stay out here if you want, but I'm going back in," James said.

He was already turning away when the light on his phone went out, leaving them in darkness. "Weird—must have run out of battery," he said, shaking his phone, trying to turn it back on. "So annoying. I swear it was charged up a few minutes ago." He sighed and tucked it into his pocket. "Anyway—don't stay out too long. See you back inside."

Remi slumped her shoulders as her brother vanished into the

shadows. She stretched out the arms of her sweatshirt so they covered her cold hands, then sat down on the grass alone with her thoughts, listening to the endless drone of the crickets. Had James been right? Was her life so devoid of excitement that her brain was making up its own stories now? She frowned at the thought.

A rustling noise came from the trees beyond the pond. Remi quickly scrambled to her feet and peered around, her senses heightened. It was probably just a squirrel or a possum, but she had heard stories of mountain lions, and suddenly she regretted being out here alone. Her fear of the skeletal hand had made her heedless of more ordinary dangers.

But as she looked over the orchard, it wasn't a possum or mountain lion she saw, but an apparition, garish white—the color of a sickly moon. It staggered through the trees, its light flickering dimly as it moved between breaks in the canopy. It was limping, dragging itself along across the dirt.

Then it stopped.

Bright green eyes turned in her direction.

Remi's instincts told her to run—but she didn't. She approached the figure in a half trance, frozen grass crunching beneath her boots. The form began to rise and take shape before her, and then—

✕✕✕

"Remi?"

A spark of consciousness re-formed in her mind, the tiniest grain of awareness. Her thoughts twisted around the kernel like threads of yarn wrapping a spool, and as they grew, she came to remember herself, but only vaguely. Something pushed back against her being, stifling her mind, brushing aside her thoughts.

"Remi?"

The voice was closer now. Familiar. Now it was her mind that pushed back, making room for the spool to grow.

"Please wake up!"

The world snapped into place.

Remi opened her eyes and found her little sister leaning over her. She was three years younger, with long black hair, braided and pulled back. Her eyes were pools of misty blue.

"Are you okay?"

She heard the concern in her sister's voice, saw it in her face, and knew something was wrong.

"Liv?"

Something splashed down on her cheek. A tear. Her sister sniffled and wiped her eyes. When Liv finally pulled back, Remi saw the stars overhead and felt the cold, damp air that had settled into her bones while she slept.

She rubbed her eyes and sat up, and to her surprise her little sister lunged forward and threw her arms around her, hugging her so tight her breath escaped her. Liv's wet cheek pressed against her own.

"It's good to see you too," Remi said. Still trying to figure out what had happened, she tried hard not to panic. "What—what are you doing down here?"

Her sister ignored her and continued to hold her tight. Then, after a long pause, she let go. "I should ask you the same thing! I followed you and James out of the house. I hid so you wouldn't see me, and then James left, and the next thing I knew you were gone. I heard something by the trees, like an explosion or something, and came looking for you down here. That's when…" She wiped her eye. "That's when I found you lying on the ground."

Liv pulled her legs up and tucked her knees beneath her chin. "You scared the heck out of me. Your eyes were open, but you weren't moving. I thought you were…" Her voice quivered. "Sorry, I know I shouldn't talk like that."

Remi dug her fingers into her forehead, massaging away the headache that was forming. She felt terrible, but tried to hide it from her sister. "I'm okay, really."

Liv snapped, "I don't believe you! Why are you lying on the ground then? Something happened to you—I know it!"

"I'm fine," Remi said. "You're getting to be as bad as Mom and Dad."

"Okay, then tell me what happened."

"I honestly don't know." Remi frowned and looked around, puzzling over how she'd ended up here. "I saw something floating on the pond earlier tonight. Some kind of strange light. I called James outside after dinner to look at it. But it was gone by the time we got to the water, so he went back inside, thinking I was making the whole thing up. Then... then there was something moving under the trees. Some kind of weird lights. I went to see what they were. And..." *And then what?* She couldn't remember. She reached for the memory, but there was nothing there.

She shook her head. "And the next thing I knew, I woke up here—with you standing over me." She took a breath. "It sounds crazy, right?"

Her sister eyed her suspiciously, then nodded. Somehow, she looked even more worried.

"Look..." Remi said. "I know I sound insane. I tried to tell James earlier, but he didn't believe me."

"Of course he didn't—he only cares about himself. He's inside watching TV instead of doing his homework. He'll be lucky if he doesn't flunk out of school this year."

Remi laughed, then her face grew serious. "I need to ask you a favor," she said. "Something very important."

"What?"

"You know how Mom and Dad can be. If they find out about this, they'll worry themselves to death and never let me outside again. This is between you and me. Our secret—okay?"

She hated asking, given how much her sister looked up to her. It felt dishonest. But she knew she was telling the truth: her parents really would freak out.

She studied her sister's face, waiting for her reaction.

At last, Liv replied. "I guess I won't say anything if you don't want me to." She hugged Remi again. "Just promise that you're okay. I don't want you to be sick again. I need you." She started to cry again, and hid her face.

"Liv?" Remi pulled her sister's hands away from her face, but Liv shook her head and stared at the ground. "Liv? I promise you I'm okay." She lifted her sister's head up and wiped away the tears with her thumb. "Look at me—I'm fine. See?" She doubted the words as she spoke them, waited for her sister to protest, but Liv merely nodded.

Remi pulled herself up slowly, then reached a hand down to her sister, who accepted it, still sniffling. "And don't tell James either. The last thing I need is him making fun of me. Come on, get up." She squeezing her sister's hand tightly to let her know she was okay.

Liv laughed again and dried her eyes. Remi put her arm around her, pulling her close by her side, and they walked back to the house.

CHAPTER 2
THE LONELIEST COMPANION

REMI DREAMED THAT NIGHT of a place she'd never been, of things she'd never seen. She stood on the polished floors of a factory room, surrounded by endless rows of white plastic bodies that stretched into the distance and vanished in a point. The robots glistened eerily under the overhead lights, each one without flaw.

She couldn't tell one robot from the next. Smooth oval masks concealed their faces, if they had them at all. They had no mouths either, no noses, just almond glass eyes that reflected the bodies around them like cold dark mirrors, each stare as empty as the next.

But then one of the faces began to change. An emerald spark lit behind the glass eyes, bathing the room in green light. A loud hiss came from behind it, and the harness around its waist released. The robot stepped forward from its rank, turned, and looked in her direction. The overhead lights faded, and she felt a sudden fear spread through her.

The robot walked slowly toward her. As it moved, the plastic mask began to melt away, peeling back like burning paper, revealing layers of circuits and wires, then a face underneath. She tried to get a better look, but couldn't make it out.

Closer.

The face began to take shape.

Another step—

She saw *herself* beneath the dissolving mask. Her hazel eyes glowed a bright green, casting a garish tint over her freckled complexion. The phantom spoke to her, but it was not her voice.

"Find her. Find Alethea."

✘✘✘

Remi sat at her kitchen table, gazing out the window and sketching on her tablet. The midday sun hid behind clouds, taking the warmth and color of the world with it; the sky was almost as lifeless and dull as she felt today. She was supposed to be doing schoolwork, but she couldn't stop thinking about what had happened the night before.

The whole idea seemed ridiculous: she and Duke finding a floating dome on the pond. But it was what she saw next that troubled her the most: the pale figure with green eyes moving under the trees. She must have imagined it, yet she felt certain of what she had seen. It had to be real. Didn't it?

She remembered walking toward the figure… and nothing more. The next thing she knew she was in the orchard, with Liv waking her up. Everything in between was missing. She must have fallen asleep after James left, dozed off. It was the only explanation. But why? She hadn't felt particularly tired.

She wished she could remember what happened.

And then there was the other matter: her dream. She hardly ever remembered them, but this one—way more vivid and brilliant than usual—had startled her awake and left her exhausted. She was still haunted by the vision of that robot with her face. And that name…

Alethea.

She rested her chin in her hand and continued to draw on her tablet, puzzling over the events.

Across the table, her mother looked up from her notes. "You okay, Remi? You seem off today, spacey or something. Feeling all right?" The question hung in the air.

Remi set her stylus and tablet down. She tried to appear relaxed, though she knew her mom would see through it. "Just have a massive head—" She caught herself. "Everything's fine—I'm just tired."

Her mom squinted and looked suspiciously at her daughter. She picked up the tablet and examined Remi's work. Frowning, she looked up. "What in the world are these?" she asked, swinging the tablet around so Remi could have a look.

The screen was filled with slashes and circles: ones and zeroes.

01011111010000010101001001010100010010011001
01000110010001010101011000010111110010000000
01001101010000001010100110101010100 01000101...

It continued on, page after page, more of the same.

Remi stared at the screen in total disbelief. "Huh."

"*Huh?* That's the best you've got?"

"Did I write that?"

"Obviously you wrote it. It's your handwriting, isn't it? And I've been watching you scribble these patterns, or whatever they are, for the last hour now."

Remi knew she must have written the numbers, but she hadn't been aware of doing it. She felt unsettled by it, and tried to cover it up. "They're not patterns, Mom. It's binary." Seeing the confused look on her mother's face, she continued, "Computer code."

Her mom rolled her eyes. "I'm going to start taking your games away if you can't focus on your work."

"It's not because of my games, Mom. I have no idea what it means—or why I wrote it. They're just doodles, I guess." She tried to play it off, but inside she was wondering if it had something to do with the night before.

"Well, next time, more working, less doodling, if you don't mind," said her mom. "Anyway, right now I need to run a few errands in town. We're running low on food, and you know how James gets when he's hungry. Do you mind holding the fort down for an hour or two?"

Remi liked the idea of having some time to herself. If nothing else, it would give her a chance to try to figure out what had happened last night. She couldn't shake the feeling that something was wrong.

"Sure, Mom." And like a broken record, she said what she had said so many times before: "I'll be okay."

She kissed her mom goodbye and turned back to the window. A short while later, she saw her mom's car disappear under the swaying pines that lined the driveway. It would still be a few hours before James and Liv got home from school, and, like every day, Remi had time to kill—way too much of it. It wouldn't be like this forever, she knew, but the day when she was allowed to go back to regular school, allowed to feel normal again, couldn't come soon enough.

She let her gaze wander up the mountains that climbed steeply from the valley where they lived. Her attention was drawn to one peak in particular, where a broad area near the top was scarred and bare without trees. She remembered a night, almost two years ago, when she had watched the flames ravage that area. The embers' smoldering aura had lasted through the night, and the smoke had settled across the peaks the next morning.

The forest fire had made the local news, of course, but the authorities didn't offer up many details—which had allowed rumors to grow like weeds in the cracks. Two boys—brothers, she'd heard—were responsible. No one was sure how it started. But some claimed to have seen a massive silver eagle—far too large to be anything from nature—soaring from the mountains and over the town, with white eyes that shone for miles. People thought the brothers had built the creature by attaching large wings to some kind of drone, like a flying Frankenstein. And, as kids sometimes do, they had crashed it—right into a tree, starting the fire. Their family moved away shortly thereafter, taking the truth with them.

But Remi had seen things after that—during her "reprogramming." That's what she called it. It was a word she had heard one night in the hospital, while eavesdropping on a conversation between a doctor and her parents when they thought she was asleep. The doctor said that in order to fight back against her disease, her immune system would need to be reprogrammed to go on the attack—to seek and destroy. Just like a machine, a computer. Modify its code. And that's exactly what the doctors did: they modified her. It worked, but it meant feeling even worse than before while her body fought back.

During her stays in the hospital, in the earliest hours of the morning, when she awoke from the late-night fevers, sheets damp and hair slick, her body and mind aching deeply, she would stare out at the mountainside and let her mind escape her room and drift with the stars, wandering freely in the shadowland. This was a world where time ceased to be—everything frozen and still. These were the loneliest times. Even with her mom or dad asleep in the chair beside her bed, lulled to sleep by the rhythmic beeps of the hospital machines, she felt like the last person alive.

And every so often, she would see them: twin specks of faraway light that moved in graceful unison across the hills. Nocturnal spirits from another world, bound together, forever. They comforted her, whatever they were; they told her she wasn't alone. She would watch them move and sway until she eventually grew tired and fell asleep.

And then, at last, she was released from the hospital, her disease nearly defeated. She hadn't seen those spirits since.

The lights could have been a hallucination, a fever dream. That was the most reasonable explanation. But she believed in what she had seen. And that was all that mattered. Those lights were real, just like her experience last night had been real. Somehow, she would get to the bottom of this. She would retrace her steps and figure this out.

Remi threw on a coat, let the dog out, and stepped out the back door. The world was cold and quiet, the air heavy, with an unusual stillness. She zipped up her coat, shoved her hands in her pockets, and trudged down her back yard to the pond, hoping to find some kind of clue as to what had happened. Apart from the slender willow leaves that fell onto the water, nothing stirred.

She walked around to the opposite side of the pond, where the old willow grew, and gazed across the orchard below. She had an eerie unsettling feeling, as if something wasn't right. But she shook her head, insisting to herself that nothing was there, and headed down the hill into the trees—just to prove to herself that her uneasiness was nonsense.

She had wandered for a bit when she spotted a line of ash in the dirt underneath an apple tree. And just beyond it—

Her breath caught.

It was the glowing dome she had seen floating on the pond. Only now, its light was extinguished, leaving it colorless and dull. It reminded her of one of those jellyfish bells she used to find washed ashore on the beach. Fallen leaves had blown into a pile around it.

She knelt down beside the strange object, careful not to get too close. All day, she had tried to convince herself that she was going crazy—that she had imagined the entire thing. But here was proof, right in front of her.

She reached out to touch it, hesitating as her finger neared its surface. Where did this thing come from? Another world? Maybe it would do something horrendous to her. Her arm might fall off—or worse.

She pulled her hand back, grabbed a stick instead, and cautiously poked at the object. The end of the stick pushed into the spongy plastic, but the dome bounced right back into form when she pulled the stick away. And nothing happened to the stick—it didn't go up in smoke, vaporize, or catch fire.

Remi reached out again, this time with her hands, to pick it up. But as soon as she lifted it off the ground, it began to shake violently. With a shriek, she dropped it and jumped back.

The dome rattled across the dirt. A light appeared inside it, faint, but warming quickly. The dome stopped moving, and the light dimmed and brightened, pulsing with the slow rhythm of a heartbeat.

She felt the light pulling her forward.

Drawing her in.

Flashing in time. Just like those eyes.

Those eyes.

Her mind grew foggy, and the world spun around her. The sky twisted, and what little color it held bled away, leaving a dark void of nothing in its place. Day yielded to starless night, and an electric frost swept over the ground, infinite streams of silver particles that swirled in the dirt and grass like tiny eddies. A breeze rustled through the trees, the crystal leaves tearing from the branches. Remi watched them drift away in the wind, followed their graceful somersaults, before they scraped the ground and took flight once more.

Standing there, captivated by their movement, she felt a presence behind her.

She whipped around and found herself gazing at a distant light: a bright, flickering star. It grew larger, and she knew it was coming toward her. She felt afraid, alone—but then the fear vanished, and a warmth settled over her. She no longer saw the light as a star, but rather as something much more: thousands of triangles, violet, purple, and white, drifting and turning in the air like shards of glass in the cold vacuum of space, loosely woven together into the form of a woman.

The spirit glided toward her. Magnificent wings carried her effortlessly through the sky with but a whisper of sound. When she reached Remi, she looked down and smiled, floating just above the earth, and Remi was mesmerized by the shifting angles that formed the woman's face.

The woman reached out her hand. *Come with me...*

Where are we going? Remi wondered, her mind absent of reason. But before she could move, she felt something buzzing on her side, breaking the spell.

My phone.

The world returned to normal.

Flustered, Remi pulled the phone from her pocket, her hands shaking. She figured it was a text from her mom, but instead she saw a strange message on the screen, blinking in time with the dome:

> Host body missing: Identifying suitable replacement.

The message vanished almost immediately, and in its place, the phone displayed image after image. They whizzed by, too quickly for Remi to even identify what they were, much less understand what they meant. She shook her phone, trying to make sense of what was happening. Somehow, she understood that the object on the ground—the dome—was controlling it, but she didn't know how.

And then the buzzing stopped, and the screen went blank.

Remi looked down at the dome. It, too, was no longer glowing. She reached for it, and it felt cool to the touch.

Her phone shook in her hands once again, startling her so much she nearly dropped it. The "new message" icon had bloomed above her messaging app.

One new message. No, three. No, ten—the counter was climbing fast. When it stopped, Remi had over thirty new messages waiting for her, each one saying the same thing:

> Order placed. Instant delivery selected.

Her eyes grew wide.

> Estimated arrival time: NOW

CHAPTER 3

MIDNIGHT MAKER

ON HER FRONT PORCH, Remi turned the dome over in her hands, running her fingers against its spongy surface. Through the translucent plastic, she could barely make out tangles of wires that formed delicate branches within. So many of them, she thought, losing herself in the intricate structures. Where did this thing come from?

She set the dome on the step and wondered what to do next. She considered showing it to James, to prove she was right all along, but then what? He'd run straight to their parents. Maybe she could show it to Liv? No, Liv already had enough secrets to keep; she didn't deserve the burden.

She decided to keep this to herself for now. At least it would give her something to do while her brother and sister were at school. Something interesting, for once.

Her thoughts were interrupted by a buzzing sound. It was far off, but growing louder by the second, and it was coming from above.

She looked up to see a squadron of electronic delivery drones approaching her house. They filled the sky like an army of giant locusts, blades humming, boxes suspended by claws that hung beneath them. She watched in amazement as they gathered in the driveway, and in a coordinated movement, assembled into a line. One by one, they deposited their packages on the porch. Then they retracted their claws and drifted off into the sky, leaving Remi alone with a mountain of boxes.

She took a look at the shipping addresses. After what she had seen on her phone earlier, she wasn't surprised to find that they were all made out to her. She had no idea what they contained—wasn't sure she *wanted* to know—but whatever it was, she was certain it was not something she wanted to explain to her parents. Or James. There was only one thing to do.

She lugged the boxes into the house, up the stairs, and into the attic. No one had been up there in years, so she knew the packages would be safe from prying eyes.

When at last all of the packages were tucked away in the attic, she stood on a small square of plywood—the only area of the floor that remained uncovered—wiped the sweat from her forehead, and watched the dust flitter down through the afternoon light onto a sea of cardboard.

But just as she went to open the first box, she heard the sound of the school bus barreling down the street. James and Liv would be here in only a few minutes. Frustrated, she looked over the boxes one last time, wondering what mysteries lay inside. She was so close to getting an answer. But she would have to wait a little longer.

She folded up the attic stairs and closed the door behind her.

)O(O(

That night, Remi paced around her room, waiting impatiently for everyone to fall asleep. Her dad was usually the last one awake, watching his shows just before bed. They seemed to drag on forever tonight, and she grew more anxious with each passing second. But finally, the noise of the television was replaced by the roar of her father's snores, and she slipped out of her room.

The springs in the attic stairs groaned when she pulled them down from the ceiling. She paused, frozen, until she was convinced she hadn't woken anyone; then she climbed up.

The attic had one window at the end, where the slanted roof joined, and it let in a long square of moonlight. Remi had never been up here at night. Strange how normal things could seem so much more sinister in the dark. She stomached her fear and pulled the stairs closed behind her.

Eager to escape the imaginary terrors lurking in the gloom, she found the chain for the overhead bulb and turned it on. The boxes cast shadows that rocked in time with the swaying bulb.

Time for some answers, she thought.

She'd already decided which box she would open first: the largest one. She tore into it as though it were an enormous present. Rummaging through the Styrofoam, she found a glass and metal cube. It had rails at the top and a small cylindrical device that moved between them. It was too heavy to lift, so she tilted the box on its side and slid it out in an avalanche of foam peanuts.

A 3D printer!

She had seen them at school, but this one looked newer—and way more expensive.

Remi found an outlet and plugged it in. The lights on the printer warmed, and the motors hummed softly.

But as exciting as it was to have a 3D printer, she wasn't sure what to do with it. So she started unpacking the rest of the boxes. These contained an odd assortment of metal and plastic parts, some with sleek curves, others with mechanical innards and trailing wires. Before long, the floor looked like some kind of high-tech assembly line.

The last box she opened, and one of the smallest, contained a pair of Orbature augmented reality glasses. Finally, something she knew how to use. She pulled them from their case, powered them on, and slid them over her eyes. Immediately her phone buzzed in her pocket—connecting to the glasses.

And then, in her vision, the room came alive. All around her, the parts began to flash, one after the next. Glowing horizontal lines moved up and down each object, then disappeared, replaced by the word "identified." After all the parts had been scanned, more text appeared, directly in front of Remi:

"Instructions downloaded. Begin assembly."

This night was getting stranger by the second.

An arrow of light bounced atop a pile of loose parts. One of the boxes had contained nothing but these twisty bits of metal, plastic, and other materials, and she had just dumped them out. But now, through the glasses, one particular spool wrapped in silver strands began to flash—and when she picked it up, it glowed. She read the label that hovered in the air above it: *printer filament.*

Now what?

She looked around the attic again. The bouncing arrow pointed to the 3D printer.

She looked down at the spool, then back at the printer. *Hmm. I guess it wants me to put this in there.*

As she studied the printer, a button flashed near the top of the cage. She pressed it, and a drawer opened on the printer's side. With the glasses guiding her way, she loaded the spool into the drawer and fed the end of the silver strand into a tube. Then she closed the drawer.

Immediately the printer's arm swung into action. It moved in rhythmic patterns, creating layers of plastic. Remi waited for it to finish, then removed the printed object and turned it over in her hand. It looked like... part of a finger?

The printer whirred and began printing again. A minute later, Remi was holding what was clearly the rest of that same finger. She could see that the two pieces fit together, but there was no snap, no connector, no glue.

She looked around the room, hoping for guidance from the

bouncing arrow. But this time, instead of the arrow, glowing rings appeared over some of the parts, with glowing numbers hovering just above them.

One… Two… Three…

Remi gathered the parts, her socks muffling her steps.

Steel bearings.

Colored wires.

A small motor.

When she had completed her list, she looked around the attic once more.

Her glasses gave her no further instructions.

Confused, she set all her items on the floor and examined them. And then the glasses responded. Holographic directions appeared in the air, overlaid on each part: numbers, arrows, even moving images of pieces fitting together. Following the instructions, Remi picked up a bearing and connected it to the first finger joint.

It popped into place.

Jackpot.

The worry that had consumed her all afternoon was beginning to fade. She was having fun in spite of everything that had happened, watching her creation come to life. Whatever the heck it was.

The glasses lit with more directions.

She knew what to do…

XOXOX

Several hours later, hands on her hips, she stood marveling over a half-assembled robot arm. She had experience with electronics from her junior robotics class, but she'd never seen anything like this. Nothing even close. This looked like it had come from another world. And maybe it had.

The printer motors were still humming when the attic door popped open, startling her. Liv's eyes appeared above the floor, searching the room. "Hey, I—"

"Shhhh," Remi hissed. She ran over and pulled Liv into the room, blanket trailing behind her, and closed the door. "You nearly scared me to death. What are you doing up?"

"What am *I* doing up?" Liv looked hurt. "I was going to ask you the same thing. I couldn't sleep, so I came into your room to talk. But you weren't there." She wrapped herself in her blanket and scanned the room. "What in the—"

Remi shot her a look. "Just calm down."

"Calm down? I knew something was going on with you. Where did all this stuff come from?" Liv's voice grew louder by the second.

"I'm not saying anything until you settle down. You'll wake up the whole house. Can you let me talk for a minute?"

Her sister nodded.

"Okay," Remi said. "The truth is, I don't know for sure…"

Her sister glared at her.

"But I have an idea. You know where you found me lying on the ground under the trees? Well, yesterday I went back there, and I found this strange glowing object on the ground—the same one I saw in the pond the other night. I touched it, and the next thing I knew, my phone started going crazy. Then it stopped, and I literally had pages of emails of stuff that had been ordered on my Amazon account. The next thing I knew, the delivery drones were dropping all this stuff off." She waved her hand around the room.

Liv's eyes moved to the glasses on Remi's head. "Are those Orbatures? I've been wanting a pair of those!" She reached out for them, but Remi pulled back.

A tapping sound made them both look down. The robot arm had started inching its way across the floor, its fingers marching against the plywood like a spider. A tangle of wires dragged behind it.

"Okaaaay," Liv said, backing away. "That's the creepiest thing I've ever seen."

The hand bumped into a wall, turned around, and began crawling in the opposite direction.

Liv picked up a large rubber tread and examined it.

"Put that down!" Remi snapped.

Liv dropped it and slumped to the floor with a pout. "What are you making, anyway?"

Remi ignored the question. The printer had just completed a new set of parts, and she began putting them together. When she looked up a few minutes later, Liv was curled up in her blanket, asleep.

Remi padded softly over to her sister and kissed her on the forehead.

Then she returned to her work.

CHAPTER 4

STRANGE AWAKENING

THE NEXT FEW nights were more of the same. Remi would wait until the house fell quiet, then sneak back into the attic and continue her project, working diligently until the early hours of the morning. She was able to squeeze in a few hours of sleep here and there, but not nearly enough. She was so exhausted she could barely connect two wires together. It didn't matter though; the further she went, the more curious she became. It was like putting a puzzle together without the picture on the box—she had no idea what she was building. But the parts continued to disappear from the floor, finding their way into the machine. It came together splendidly, guided by the strange program inside her phone and glasses.

Now, with dawn's light creeping in through the window, she surveyed the floor, looking for the next part. There was nothing left. She sat down, swept a pile of boxes out of her way, and marveled at her work. Not too bad, she thought, smiling to herself. She dusted her hands off. Not bad at all.

Her glasses lit once more. A holographic dome materialized before her: one last step.

Feeling a rush of exhilaration, she crept down the stairs and woke Liv. Together, they managed to haul the machine down to Remi's room without waking anyone.

Remi pulled the dome from her dresser drawer where she had hidden it. Then, with Liv watching intently, she turned back toward her creation and made the final connection.

XOXOX

Remi and Liv stared at the machine. It was a bit larger than a shoebox, shaped like a tank, with rubber treads on each side that wrapped around gearhead motors. The dome sat in the center, and just behind it was the robotic arm, bent steeply at the joint in the middle, so that the arm reached forward like a scorpion's tail, fingers dangling. A speaker was mounted on the front between the treads, with red and black wires running through holes in the silver chassis, and right above the speaker was a camera. Its eyes, Remi figured.

The morning sun shone through the window, and the robot sparkled in the light.

"Now what?" Liv asked.

Remi studied the machine, unmoving on the carpet. There was no on-and-off switch—at least none that she knew of. "I don't know," she replied.

Then she remembered the battery she had wired up inside the chassis. Her phone always needed to be charged; maybe this did, too. Crouching down, she found a socket on the side.

"I think we have to plug it in. Hold on a sec. I have an idea." Remi crept back to the attic, remembering something she had seen earlier, buried among the boxes. She was back in her room a minute later holding a power cord.

"Got it!"

She plugged one end of the cord into the wall, and was pleased to see the other fit smoothly into the robot's socket. She stepped back and waited.

Nothing happened.

"Maybe you missed a step," Liv said.

Remi glared sideways at her. "I don't think—"

A ridiculously loud yawn came from James's room, followed by footsteps across the hall into the bathroom, then the sound of a running faucet. The giant had stirred.

"Oh great—James is up," Remi said. "Come on, help me hide this thing."

They shoved the creation into the mess that was Remi's closet, leaving the cord winding under the closet door to the outlet. Then they headed downstairs for breakfast.

After nearly falling asleep face down in her cereal, Remi told her Mom she wasn't feeling well, stumbled back up the stairs, and found her way to bed.

XXX

When she opened her eyes, Remi found herself peering over a steel table, wondering where she was and how she'd gotten here. She felt detached from herself once again, as if her consciousness had been pushed aside to make room for another. She was only half aware, watching the world through someone else's eyes…

Dreaming someone else's dream.

A light shone over her shoulder, illuminating a robot that lay on the table. It had the same white plastic mask as the robot from her dream, but this one was different. It was much smaller than the others.

A child?

Her arms came from around her sides. Or at least, they felt like her arms, but she knew they didn't belong to her. These were robot arms, covered in white plastic, and they held tools that moved gracefully over the child. Lights flashed and the plastic glistened as the arms that weren't hers went about their work.

A hand moved toward the child's head, turning it to the side, then the other hand came around with a different tool. As it made contact, a quick, high-pitched whistle sounded, and the small robot's eyes began to glow.

The child sat up slowly, green eyes blazing. Remi's hands reached out and picked up the robot underneath its arms, lifting it up toward the overhead lights. A wonderful sense of joy and pride came over her—some of the happiest feelings she had ever felt. She knew the memory and the emotions belonged to someone else, but she was happy too. She gazed up at the robot, feeling prouder than ever.

Then the voice that wasn't her own spoke.

"Welcome to the world, my son."

XXXX

A sound in the closet woke her. Stiff and robotic, muffled behind the closed door.

"Voice circuits enabled. Ninety percent charged."

Charging… ninety… zzzz, Remi thought, drool pooling in the corner of her mouth. She closed her eyes and pulled her pillow over her ears.

The robotic voice droned on.

"Ninety-one percent charged."

Please, shut up. She just wanted to sleep.

"…Ninety-three…"

Oh, for goodness' sake. She sat up and tossed her pillow at the closet door.

Her room was dark. Head pounding, she went for her phone and checked the time.

Just past midnight.

How is it so late?

And then the dreary fog of sleep lifted. She remembered her mom scanning a thermometer across her forehead and the door closing softly behind her when she left. She panicked at the realization that she'd slept the entire day away. How in the world would she explain this?

She reached over to her nightstand to set her phone down, but she stuck her phone, and her hand, into something soft. She turned on her lamp to see what it was: mashed sweet potatoes, piled high, roasted chicken, and a slice of chocolate pie off to the side: her favorite.

There was also a note.

Missed you at dinner—hope you're feeling better.

Love, Mom. xoxo.

Guilt rose in her throat. Her parents must have been worried sick about her all day. She still had a few weeks left before her final treatment, one last stay in the hospital, doctors and nurses buzzing around her like bees. And until then, her parents were watching her like a hawk, looking for anything even slightly wrong—a high temperature, a chill in the night, anything.

This would sound alarms.

Remi wiped the potatoes off her phone and eyed the plate hungrily, her gaze settling on the chocolate pie. *Well, the mashed potatoes can wait,* she thought as she picked up the slice.

Just as she was going to take a bite, a rattling sound came from the closet. She remembered the voice that had woken her.

Scowling, she set the pie down, opened the closet door, and swept the hangers aside.

The robot's dome glowed softly, pulsing, like it had in the pond. Something must have activated it. Or maybe it had activated itself.

A voice came from the speaker, loud and clear this time.

"Ninety-nine percent charged. Beginning emergency boot sequence."

Boot sequence? Remi poked her head in to get a closer look. The dome pulsed faster.

"Fully charged. Boot complete. Personality matrix engaged."

She crept even closer.

"Screeeeee!"

Remi jumped back and shrieked, slamming the door on the bot. Obviously, connecting the speaker had been a mistake.

The noise stopped after only a few seconds, but Remi was still reluctant to open the door, for fear she would set it off again. Maybe if she moved quickly, she could disconnect the wires from the speaker before it woke anyone.

She waited a minute, then another. The house was dead quiet. At least no one had been woken yet.

She eyed the door suspiciously, then inched her hand toward the knob. She turned it, cautiously, opening it just a crack, and then—

The door exploded open.

The bot lurched forward, past her feet, and slammed straight into her closed bedroom door.

"Screeeeee!"

This time Remi was ready. She yanked out the wire that connected the speaker, and the room fell silent.

The bot turned toward her, its camera glaring at her like an angry eye, then it turned back to face the bedroom door. To Remi's amazement, its arm rose up, turned the knob, and opened the door, and the bot rolled forward into the dark hallway. The sounds of its motors echoed in the stillness of the house.

"Get back here!" Remi hissed.

The bot continued on, its arm flailing about.

Remi followed, moving softly in her socks, and grabbed the bot before it could tumble down the stairs. Its rubber treads revved and squeaked against the floor. "Not so fast," she whispered, scooping it up. Now the treads whizzed in midair.

A cough came from her parents' bedroom, and she heard a break in her father's snores. She paused to see if he had woken up. But the lights stayed off, and after a few seconds, his snoring resumed.

She crept down the stairs, bot in her arms, and found Duke

waiting at the bottom, eyeing them both suspiciously. "Go back to sleep," she said, setting the bot on the ground so she could rub the dog behind the ears.

She should have known better.

The bot sped off, treads bumbling across the floor, making straight for the mudroom. She chased after it, Duke at her side, but not fast enough to stop it from opening the back door and driving straight out onto the deck.

What on earth?

Remi threw on a coat over her pajamas, stuffed her feet into boots, and went after it, closing the door behind her on a very disappointed Duke.

Apparently the bot could handle stairs after all—or perhaps it had simply tumbled down them—because its pulsing head was already halfway down the hill toward the pond.

She hurried after it. The bot's light was easy to follow in the darkness, but surprisingly hard to keep up with.

The bot moved rapidly down the hill, around the pond, and then down again toward the orchard. It slowed when it hit the trees, bumping awkwardly across exposed roots, and finally, Remi caught up to it. She lifted it from the ground, its treads still spinning, and turned its camera to face her.

"Where are you going?" she asked.

The bot's arm reached forward and shook its speaker, which still dangled by its wire.

"You want to say something, do you?" Remi said. "If I hook it back up, do you promise to keep it down?"

Remi felt silly speaking to an oversized toy, but the arm moved up and down in agreement.

She set the bot on the ground and reattached the wire. "Okay then. Can we go back inside now?" Remi cinched her hood tight and shivered.

The speaker crackled. "She's coming for me."

The hairs on Remi's neck stood up. The stiff, robotic voice from earlier was gone. This voice sounded like the voice of a child.

She leaned closer, staring into the camera. "Excuse me—what did you say?"

"She's coming for me. We have to get far away from here."

The emotion in the young voice startled her. It was worried and afraid.

It spoke again, urgently. "Hurry. We're running out of time."

She opened her mouth to say something, but stopped when she heard a loud crack. Looking up, she saw a blue light appear over the pond.

"What in the—"

The bot spoke again. "It's too late. She's found me."

CHAPTER 5

AUTO-ESCAPE

A WHISTLING CAME from high above in the cold autumn air, hollow and shrill. A ball of rusted metal drifted across the sky, its glass center glowing red, casting streaks of light over the hill.

A floating eye, Remi thought.

Its beams flashed over the grass. It scanned the ground in rows, as if methodically searching, and given what the bot had said, she knew that whatever this thing was doing here, it wasn't good.

"What in the world *is* that?" she asked.

The robot was quiet.

"Nice time to finally keep your mouth shut," she muttered under her breath.

Three more of the eyes appeared from across the trees, just like the first. They spread out, their beams weaving across the ground.

"Oh no…"

The bot's treads spun up, and it lurched forward, nearly knocking Remi off her feet as it whizzed past.

"Wait!" Remi cried.

She chased after the bot, avoiding the javelins of red light piercing through the leaves. She and the bot fled from the trees, up the bank, and around the pond. But as she ran up the hill, one of the eyes sped out in front of her, blocking her way forward.

Remi turned, but another sphere was just behind her, drawing closer. Two more orbs drifted in from her left and right. She was surrounded. Surrounded and suddenly very afraid.

She turned slowly, holding her arms out to the sides, as if that would keep them away. The eyes fell into orbit around her, matching her movements. Finally she stopped, forced to catch her breath. One of the eyes drifted up to her and faced her, head on.

The mechanical iris shifted back and forth erratically, then locked into place. The pupil dilated, and through the glass, she could see shadows, silhouettes of crumbling walls, with jagged edges against fiery skies. She felt as though she could reach out and touch them. They flickered in and out.

The floating orb came closer, hovering mere inches away from her face. Something else now moved behind the eye's curved glass: a shadowy cloud that emerged from the ruins. The dark mass grew larger, moving toward Remi, and a hooded form took shape—slender, with a long, heavy coat covering its body. One of its sleeves was missing, the fabric torn from the shoulder, exposing an arm formed of wires, pistons, and rusted metal plates. It moved with an eerie gracefulness.

Remi stepped to the side, trying to escape the figure's gaze, but the orb moved with her.

Soon she was face-to-face with the creature behind the glass. Its cowl was old and torn, and beneath the hood was a visor with two glass eyes that tapered to sharp points, shining red. A threadbare scarf covered its mouth.

"Where is he?" Its voice was rough and garbled.

She had no idea what it was talking about. "I don't understand!"

The thing in the eye moved closer, its face filling the glass.

"I said—where is he?"

Behind Remi, the bot's speaker blared. *"Ruuuuunnnnn!"*

The eye snapped shut, and the orbs lifted back into the air.

Remi rubbed her eyes, trying to figure out what had just happened. She looked around for the small robot, and saw it speeding up the hill toward her house. One of the eye-orbs was following closely behind it, its red beam lighting the ground.

The bot's headed for my house—

My family! It's leading the eyes right to them!

Remi ran as fast as she could, hoping to catch the bot before it reached the door. But there was no need; one of the eyes swung down from the sky and drifted languidly in front of the back door, blocking the bot's path. The bot immediately changed course and headed toward the driveway. To Remi's surprise, her dad's car roared to life. The bot gripped the bumper tightly with its arm.

"Get in the car!" the bot shrieked.

The car began to roll down the driveway.

With no other choice, Remi ran after the car, the eyes chasing behind her. She ran alongside the moving vehicle, opened the door, and jumped into the back seat.

The car screeched out of the neighborhood, then turned onto an unlit side street, where it picked up speed. Remi spun around and saw the eyes in pursuit.

She lowered the window and poked her head out. The sky was red behind her. "Faster!" she screamed, hoping the bot was still attached. It had to be, didn't it? If it wasn't, who was in control?

The car accelerated as they raced down the main street of town. Shops passed by in a blur. Soon they had cleared the town and then the valley. The car turned onto a back road where the tops of the trees formed an arch overhead, a shadowy steeple over the asphalt. Lights blinked on the dash and reflected off the windshield.

The road began to climb, and so did their speed. Thirty—forty—fifty. She imagined the poor bot, trailing behind, sparks no doubt shooting from its treads. When they took a corner, she felt

two wheels come off the road. And still the glowing eyes continued their pursuit.

Remi glanced at the speedometer.

Sixty. I'm not going to make it!

But they went faster still, and Remi closed her eyes. The car
pitched and rolled as it climbed the mountain.

And then the car began to slow.

CHAPTER 6

OVERDRIVE

THE ENGINE'S HUM grew softer, and the car rolled to a stop, pavement grinding beneath the tires. The lights went out with the vehicle in the middle of the road—and the middle of nowhere.

Remi's heart thumped so hard she felt the blood rushing through her ears. She peeked out the rear window, her eyes following the long stretch of road that led back down the mountain, back to her home.

The eyes were nowhere to be seen.

She locked the doors and slumped down in the seat, listening to the rhythmic click of the car's flashing emergency lights.

Why did we stop? Remi asked herself. *And what do I do now?*

What had she been thinking anyway, racing away in a car piloted by some kind of alien robot? She should have said something to her parents the night she found the dome—any other sane person would have. Now it was too late. She would have to call her parents to come and get her. There would be consequences, but she would face them. Spend the rest of her life locked in her room if she had to. Her cozy, safe, and so *boring* room.

Right now, boring had never seemed so appealing.

She fumbled in her pajama pocket for her phone, scowling when she realized she had left it at home.

There had to be another way. And then... she had an idea.

The bot.

If it had driven her car here by itself—and she was pretty sure it had—maybe she could talk to it, convince it to take her home.

She opened the door and stepped out onto the pavement. The road made a sharp turn up ahead, hugging the mountain tightly. A guardrail followed the road on the other side, the few feet of rocky ground beyond it giving way to an abrupt cliff. Lights flickered in the sleepy valley below.

But Remi wasn't interested in the view.

At the back of the car, she found the robot. It lay on its side, spinning in circles, its arm pointing upward.

"What are you—"

She looked up, and her eyes widened.

Swirling high above her was a ring of eyes.

For a moment, she was paralyzed with shock, but she shook it off. There was only one thing to do.

Run for it.

"Time to go." She set the bot upright and turned to sprint down the road.

But before she could take a step, a flash of light blinded her, followed by a crack, loud and sharp. The ground shook, and her car alarm began to wail.

Remi staggered back, covering her ears. A wall of blue fire had formed across the pavement, blocking her way. It was the same blue fire she'd seen from her pond when the eyes first appeared.

A dark form stepped from the light, silhouetted in flame. Somebody—or something—was coming.

Remi sprinted to the front of the car and crouched behind the bumper. The noise from the alarm was deafening, but she had nowhere else to hide. She craned her head to peer around the side.

The firelight vanished, but the strange creature remained. It stood unmoving at the edge of the cliff, gazing out at an even larger swarm of eyes now gathering in the sky. A long brown coat covered its body, giving way to rusted metal boots. Its head was shrouded by a hood, and a robot arm hung at its side.

It was the same creature she had seen earlier, behind the crimson eye.

At least, she thought it was a creature. Its robot arm made her wonder if it was a machine—but whatever it was, seeing it in person deepened her fear of it. How had it come here? Was the blue light some kind of door—a portal into the dreadful world where it lived?

Something brushed by Remi's foot, and she jumped. But it was only the bot. "Don't be stupid. Stay put," she whispered, dropping back down.

From behind the car came the sound of steel clanking against asphalt.

"There's nowhere to run," a voice called out, raspy and low. "I don't have time to waste on you."

The footsteps grew louder, then stopped. Remi looked up and saw a red aura over the roof of her car.

"We need to go," she said, tugging at the bot's arm. She didn't know why the creature had stopped, but there was no way she was going to wait around and find out.

She slipped away from the car and crept up the road, the bot trailing behind her, surprisingly silent for once. But apparently, the darkness wasn't enough to hide them. One of the eyes moved away from the creature behind them, drifted overhead, then settled down in Remi's path, blocking her way.

They weren't going to let her go that easily.

Remi turned and found the creature waiting on the opposite side of her car. It raised its exposed arm toward the sky, and bolts of electricity flashed inside the gaps within the metal. One of the orb-eyes swirled up and around it, buzzing frantically near its fingertip. Then it cast its arm forward, and the eye hurtled toward her car.

It smashed into the side with the force of a cannonball, crushing the frame and sending it toward the guardrail, where it screeched against the metal. The guardrail bowed, groaning under the force of the car.

This can't be happening. This has to be a dream. Time to wake up, Remi Cobb!

But she knew this was no dream. She was trapped in the middle of nowhere, on a mountain road, by a robot-armed creature that commanded a legion of floating eyes.

And she was still in her pajamas.

With the car out of the way, the creature stepped toward her. Remi wanted to run, but there was nowhere left to go.

"Do you know how long I've been looking for him?" The creature stopped in front of the small robot and raised its steel boot. "Don't worry—you won't be going anywhere." It brought its foot down on one of the treads, smashing it to bits. The other tread spun uselessly.

Remi squared her shoulders and tried to sound as confident as she could, but her body was shaking. "Get away from that—it's mine."

The sight of the creature shook her. Its tattered coat and scarf were stained with dirt and grime, buttoned loosely together, and metal glinted from a tear in the fabric. Maybe it was a machine after all.

"*Yours?* Oh, no, poor child. I'm afraid not." The creature ground its toe into the remains of the broken bot, shifting it around until the electronics sizzled and popped. Bearings broke loose and spun off the side of the road.

The creature reached down and extracted the glowing dome. The eyes swarmed around like angry hornets, dodging and weaving. "I bet he thought he was clever, hiding you here, of all places."

He?

"But it didn't work. Not even he could keep you quiet—you naïve little rat. I found you the instant your mind turned on again and started wasting cycles. You'll perish just like he did. But first…"

Remi watched in horror as the tips of the creature's robot fingers folded back, revealing probes that snaked out around the dome. Then the fingers curled, and the probes tightened.

The dome pulsed so quickly it provided a near constant glow.

"I know you have the *primer code*," the creature said. "And if I have to, I'll tear your entire mind apart to get it." The probes glowed white hot. Thin traces of smoke drifted from the dome.

"Don't you dare hurt it!" Remi yelled, surprising herself.

The creature kept its gaze trained on the dome, ignoring her, the probes' light reflecting in its eyes. Then, suddenly, the probes fell slack and the dome went dark.

"It's not here!" the creature said, anger rising in its gravelly voice. It turned to Remi, still clutching the dome with its machine arm. "What have you done with it?"

"I—I have no idea what you're talking about," Remi stammered. "I don't even know what's happening here—I just want to go home."

"All that work to bring him back; all of it wasted. It's a shame you're involved with this. But—if you tell me where the code is, perhaps—"

The creature stopped midsentence and fell to its knees, pushing the palms of its hands against the sides of its head, shaking and screaming. Then it stopped and its red eyes went dark. Remi had seen many weird things tonight, but this was the strangest.

The shaking stopped, and the creature looked up at her. When it spoke, it was with a woman's voice. "You have to run from me—get away while you still can! I can't keep him out of—"

The voice broke. The eyes flickered on, their red light returning. With a shake of its head, the creature rose to its feet.

"Pardon the interruption." The ghoulish voice was back. "As I was saying, give me the code and I'll let you go."

"I already told you," Remi said. "I don't know what you're talking about."

"Have it your way, human." The creature raised its awful arm once again. Another eye broke from the sky and twisted around its finger.

Remi's world lit up with a flash.

CHAPTER 7

SOLID ROCK

THE FLASH was bright as the sun, but the heat she expected to feel never came. Raising her hand to shield her eyes, she looked up—and saw a majestic bird with searing white beams shining down from its diamond eyes. The bird dove toward her with an earsplitting screech.

Remi jumped and rolled away as the eagle soared past, its talons outstretched. It flew straight into the creature, sending it crashing to the ground, and snatched the glowing dome in its beak. After circling around once more, it lifted back into the night.

"Go!" the fallen creature screamed at the floating eyes, pointing at the bird. Two of the eyes spun off in pursuit.

Before Remi even had time to register what had happened, two more lights appeared, higher up the mountain. *Headlights.* And they were approaching fast.

An engine roared and a horn blared. Then a pickup truck squealed to a stop, and its passenger door flew open.

Finally, something she recognized, something that actually belonged in this world. Remi didn't know where that truck had come from or who was driving it, and she didn't care. Whoever was waiting behind the wheel was bound to be safer than the nightmarish robot lying on the ground. She ran for the open door.

Halfway there, she heard a click, and the cab door flew open as well. Some kind of animal leapt from the truck and bounded to the ground.

Remi skidded to a stop, eyes wide.

The animal reminded her of a Doberman, but it stood nearly twice as tall, and in place of fur, it was covered in golden bronze plates. Its eyes burned like fiery orange embers, staring right at her. And its teeth… they were easily the worst part. Jagged and bared, ready to tear something apart.

It raised its front leg, and Remi gulped as knife-like claws extended from its metal paw. Then it advanced, its nails sinking right into the asphalt.

Remi shook as the hound drew near, stunned by its size and ferocity. First she was rescued by a mechanical eagle, and now she was about to be devoured by a killer robot dog. She braced herself, waiting for it to leap at her.

But it passed right by her and moved on toward the creature.

She let out a deep sigh of relief.

The creature had pulled itself to its feet and had another one of the eyes spinning around its arm. It threw its arm forward, and the eye went speeding toward the dog.

Rather than dodging, the hound leapt right at the orb, neatly lancing it with one of its claws. The eye began to glow, and the dog flung it into the air, where it exploded in a shower of sparks.

The Doberman licked its paw and continued on.

The creature stepped backward, retreating down the road, but it was no match for the dog. The hound drew back into a crouch, then leapt at the creature, knocking it in the chest with both front paws. Both creature and dog hurtled through the air and landed on the ground near the guardrail.

Remi was so overwhelmed by all that was happening, she almost jumped out of her skin when she felt a hand on her arm.

"Come on," said a voice. "We'll be safer in the truck."

Remi found a young woman standing beside her. She was a few inches taller than Remi, with long dark hair that fell straight around her face, black pants with pockets on the sides, and a worn gray sweatshirt that was frayed around the neck and cuffs.

Remi didn't hesitate; she ran to the truck. The stranger hopped in the passenger side and slid across the seat, and Remi followed. Through the windshield, she saw the creature forcing the dog away and rising to its feet. The dog lunged at it again, but this time the creature somehow caught it and, in one fluid motion, tossed the dog over the side of the cliff.

Then the creature turned its gaze toward the truck and began walking toward them.

"We need to go," Remi said, tugging on the stranger's arm.

The woman just sat there, eyes wide and mouth agape, staring vacantly at the spot where the dog had fallen.

"Now!" Remi screamed.

The stranger shook herself, slammed her door shut, and pushed a button on the dash. The truck revved to life. She threw it into reverse and spun the wheel. Tires screeching, she wheeled the truck around and started up the road.

As Remi looked back at the robot, her eye caught movement off the side of the road—and to her shock, the dog came scurrying up over the cliff and sprinted toward them.

"Wait!" she said. "The dog—it's still alive! It's chasing us!"

The woman glanced back and, with one hand still on the wheel, reached back and opened the rear cab door with the other.

"Hurry, Achilles!" she shouted.

In a flash, the mechanical hound passed the robot and was running alongside the truck. When it jumped inside, she felt the vehicle buckle under the weight, but the truck recovered and lurched forward. Somehow, the giant hound managed to squeeze itself into the back seat.

The woman slammed the door shut and stepped on the gas just as the pavement exploded behind them.

XOXOX

The road grew steeper as they wound up the mountainside. Remi sat with one hand gripping the door, the other bracing against the dash.

"Are you okay?" the stranger asked, her eyes fixed on the road.

"Okay?" Remi replied, breathlessly. "No—that thing back there—whatever it was—just tried to kill me."

"Take a deep breath. I understand why you're scared, and I don't blame you. I'm still trying to figure out what's happening myself. I know it's hard, but it'll be easier if you try to stay calm. Just give me some time."

"You can't be serious! There are demon eyeballs floating around the sky, shooting red lasers, trying to kill us, and you expect me to stay calm?" Remi's heart thumped, and her hands shook from the adrenaline flooding her system.

"Those eyes are left over from the Neurogeists."

"*Neuro-what?*" Remi asked.

"Dreadful machines, trust me. I thought I'd seen the last of them, but it looks like someone's brought them back to life."

"Who?" Remi asked.

"I'm guessing it was that thing back there that nearly took out my best friend. But it didn't know who it was dealing with, did it?"

The dog barked loudly in the back seat, and Remi turned around and found herself face to face with the canine. It leaned forward and nuzzled its giant nose into her cheek. She could feel puffs of hot air escaping through vents on its faceplate.

"Mind telling me why there's a giant robot dog in the back seat?" Remi asked.

"His name is Achilles. Mine's Nova. I didn't catch yours."

"It's Remi. And I need to get home before my parents call the police."

The stranger named Nova glanced up at the rearview mirror. Remi watched her eyes shift back and forth, studying the road. "That's my plan. But right now we've got other problems. The eyes you mentioned—one of them is right behind us. We'll never outrun it this way. We need a different approach."

She pressed a few buttons on the dash, and for the first time, Remi noticed that the controls looked like something from the future.

"Hold on."

Nova turned the wheel hard and slammed on the emergency brake. The truck spun in the tightest turn Remi had ever taken, throwing her against the door. When they stopped, the truck was facing the mountainside.

Nova swiped the steering wheel with her thumb, and a set of new controls appeared in the center of the dash. Her fingers danced across them, and a holographic projection of the truck appeared in front of the windshield. Then the projection split in half and dissolved.

"I hope this works," Nova said.

The eye was almost upon them.

"Hope what works?" Remi asked.

"You may want to close your eyes," Nova said. "This is going to feel a little weird."

Remi stared at the solid rock that loomed before them. The truck growled. Then it dawned on her.

"You've got to be kidding!"

The stranger floored it.

The truck shot forward.

Straight into the mountain.

CHAPTER 8

NO TRESPASSING

THIS WAS THE END. Remi covered her eyes and gritted her teeth, bracing for impact.

"Hold on!" Nova shouted over the engine.

Certain death was inches away, and then—

A boom, a strange sensation, a vibration that rippled through her, then nothing more.

Remi peeked through her fingers and gasped, amazed to be alive, but not entirely sure she actually was. She couldn't believe her own eyes, didn't trust what she saw. *This can't be possible.*

Instead of crashing into the face of the mountain, the rock seemed to have *folded* around the truck, as though they were pushing through a sponge. The world around the truck was stretched, particles drifting and flowing around them in currents of space-time distortion. They moved slowly, as if even time itself had been bent, and when Remi looked out the rear window, she saw the warped rock snap back into place and wobble like a wall of jello.

A minute later, they burst from the other side of the mountain.

Nova slammed on the brakes and spun the wheel. They slid into the guardrail, and the passenger-side wheels lifted off the ground. Remi thought they would roll right over the cliff, but before they pitched over, the truck fell back down to the road, sending a cloud of dust rising from the tires.

"That should buy us a few minutes," Nova said, putting her foot on the accelerator and escaping the haze.

Remi prodded her face with her hands, making sure she was still whole. She slid her eyes over to Nova, then quickly back to the road, watching the trees pass by as they continued their climb.

"Still with me?" Nova asked.

Remi felt sick to her stomach, but was otherwise okay—somehow. She tried to find words. "Maybe." Then, after a minute: "I'm dreaming, right? What *was* that?"

"It's a quantum disrupter. It creates a field that influences the wave function to manipulate particle states."

"Sorry?"

"It moves things out of the way so they don't kill us."

"I'll… take your word for it."

"Now if you don't mind, I have a few questions of my own. For starters, what are you doing with an Artifex brain?"

"What's an Artifex brain?"

Nova sighed. "We don't have time for this."

"No, really, I'd like to help, but I have no idea what you're talking about. Please—what's an Artifex?"

"They're robots from a different world—deeply confused robots."

"Robots? What do they look like?"

"A friend of mine once said they looked like crash test dummies."

Remi recalled her nightmare from the other night. "With weird plastic faces?"

"Yes. How did you—"

"And you're telling me I had one of their brains?"

"It appears that way. And not just any brain. I've been looking for someone for a long time now, and I think I've finally found him. It's a good thing I left sensors behind to alert me if he showed up again. Last time was a real mess."

"Last time?"

"I'll explain later." Nova spun around a sharp bend, and the seat hugged Remi on the turn. "Listen to me—you're involved in something much larger than you realize. Do you have any idea what the creature was after back there?"

Remi thought back. Most of it was a blur: a life-threatening, fear-inducing, stomach-wrenching blur. But one detail stood out. "I remember it saying something about a—what was it?" She bit her lip, the words on the tip of her tongue, trying to remember. "Something about a *primer code.*"

Nova glanced at her with a look of recognition, then looked back at the road. She slowed down and turned the truck onto a narrow gravel driveway.

"Where are you taking us?"

"To see an old friend."

※※※

The tires chewed gravel as they drove deeper into the woods, still climbing. The driveway led to a cedar-shingled house, its exterior weathered and gray. The lights were off, and it looked empty. Remi wondered who had once lived there, and why they would choose to live somewhere so remote, away from everything.

The driveway stopped, but Nova drove on across the grass toward a tall metal fence at the end of the yard with a No Trespassing sign dangling by a corner. She hit the gas, and the truck rammed right through the fence, sending the sign hurtling through the air. Only then did she bring the truck to a stop.

"Was that really necessary?" Remi asked.

"Wait here," Nova said, climbing from the truck. She opened the rear cab door for Achilles, who hopped out onto the ground. Together, Nova and the dog vanished into the woods.

XXXX

Remi crept slowly from the truck, careful not to make a sound. On this clear night, the stars were brighter and crisper than she'd ever seen then before, with deep cosmic seas of purple and blue where the Milky Way swirled above. This was the mountain where the fires had burned two years ago, the place where the twin circles of light had traveled in the earliest hours of the morning. From here, she could just see the spot where the hillside was bare, ravaged by fire.

Somehow, this is all connected.

Nova had told her to stay put, but after everything she had been through tonight, she deserved answers.

She slipped into the woods, in the same spot where Nova and Achilles had disappeared. The ground cover and foliage were beginning to die with the cold air, making it easier to see between the trees.

She only walked a short way before she spotted them. Nova and her dog were standing in a clearing, and Nova was fiddling with her wristwatch. Remi hid behind a large pine and watched.

For a moment, the forest was still—then a breeze came from above, and a dark shadow glided across the sky. The eagle from before. The glowing dome—*the Artifex brain,* Remi reminded herself—was still tucked in its beak. A streak of moon-brightened silver flashed along the edges of its broad wings, and beams of white light shone from its eyes.

The lights on the mountainside, Remi thought. *They were this eagle's eyes.*

The bird arced in a circle, its cold torches passing over her. When its circle was complete, it settled on a low branch and folded its metallic wings against its body.

First the dog, now the bird; these were the most impressive creatures Remi had ever seen. But they looked far too advanced to be man-made—unless they had escaped from some super-secret high-tech lab. Nothing would surprise her at this point.

Nova approached the strange bird, and it cocked its head as if to listen. Nova smiled. "It's been a while, my friend. How are you doing?"

The creature's diamond eyes were as cold as frost. It studied her with interest.

She smiled and gestured toward the brain. "Can I have him back now?"

The bird reared back and screeched.

"No—I know. Calm down. It's okay—I know you're still upset after what he did to you. You have every right to be." Nova raised her hand toward the bird. "He can't hurt you now though—I'd say you have the upper hand."

The bird cocked its head again.

"Look, I wouldn't take him from you unless I had to. There's no other way. We have to find out what happened to him."

The eagle's white eyes flashed.

"Come on, Nyx. Let me have him. Please…?"

The bird flapped its wings once, then opened its mouth and let the brain fall from its beak. Nova caught the dome and tucked it away inside her backpack.

Remi saw no need to hide any longer. She stepped forward, toward the giant eagle. Achilles ran over and jumped around her, barking.

Nova frowned. "I asked you to stay back at the truck. Be careful around Achilles, he—"

Remi raised her hand in front of her, palm side up, and commanded, "Sit!"

The dog obeyed, gears and metal straining as he sat. He whimpered softly, looking up at her. *Waiting for a treat,* she thought, imagining the dog chewing on a tasty wrench.

Remi flashed a proud grin at Nova. "I can handle myself, thank you."

Nova shook her head. "You're determined to make this difficult, aren't you?"

Remi ignored her and approached the eagle. Its head rotated

toward her, and its eyes glimmered. "I knew you were real," she said. "I've watched you flying—late at night."

Nyx fluttered her wings, and Remi stared deep into its crystal eyes.

As she did so, a realization struck her.

To Nova, she said, "The forest fire on the mountains—two years ago. You were there, weren't you? That's what you were talking about earlier—about the last time he showed up here being a mess."

Nova nodded.

"What happened up here? What about the two boys?"

Nova looked back in the direction of the empty house. "It's a long story, but they saved my life." Her gaze followed the mountainside. "I haven't spoken to them since."

"So what do we do now?"

"For starters, we figure out how to get you home. Then *I'll* be able to return home too—hopefully with—"A buzzing overhead interrupted her, announcing the arrival of the red-eyed orbs. "They've found us."

As Nova typed furiously on her wristwatch, the spheres drifted downward, forming a circle around Remi, Achilles, Nova, and Nyx. Then they began to glow.

"Get in—now!" Nova screamed, just as a bright blue light ripped open the air in front of her. She pulled Remi forward, and the last thing Remi saw was the world bursting into flame around them.

PART 2

CHAPTER 9

HOME SWEET HOME

REMI STOOD on the side of a mountain, fragments of metal and glass crunching beneath her boots. The forest was gone, and in its place were shattered walls, jagged like mountain ranges, rising steeply around her. A large section of one of the walls was missing altogether, and through the hole, she saw the night sky. Down below, fires burned, forming hazy, orange pools of flickering light. The wind howled, and she shivered, suddenly very cold.

She thought back to the crimson world she had seen behind the lens of the floating eye, and wondered if Nova had whisked her away to that very land of ruin. The night was just as dark, the air just as cold, but everything else—everything else was impossibly different.

To her great relief, Nova and Achilles were both with her. She went to speak, but a sharp cry from above interrupted her before she had a chance. She looked up to see a dab of silver perched high on the tattered fringe of a wall. Nyx.

"You're home now," Nova called to the bird.

The bird beat its wings, lifted off with a cry, and disappeared into the clouds.

"So," Nova said to Remi. "I'm sure you have many questions."

Remi raised her eyebrows.

Questions? You'd better believe I have questions. She started with the obvious one. "What just happened to us?"

"The light we just traveled through," Nova replied, "is a quantum door. It's taken us to an alternate reality—a world like your own, yet very different. This is where Achilles and I are from. This is our reality."

"Like a parallel universe?" Remi asked.

"Kind of like that. Think of it this way: every time you are forced to make a decision, any time you move, do anything, a new reality is formed for each possible outcome. And some version of you exists in every one of them. In fact, there's no doubt one where we've never met and you're still at home in bed right now."

Home.

Remi imagined being curled up under a mountain of covers. The idea had never sounded more appealing.

Remi had many more questions, but Nova was swiping at her watch and scanning the horizon. "The door leaves a signature behind," she said. "We need to get away from here before that creature figures out where we went." She motioned down the slope. "I know a place we can hide until we can figure out how to get you home safely. Moving will help you warm up, too."

Nova started down the rough terrain, and Achilles walked at her side.

Remi had no choice but to follow. She did her best to find her footing on the uneven ground, but slipped occasionally in spite of herself, sending debris raining down the hill. Often she would catch a faint smell of smoke drifting up from below.

"I'm still not sure I understand," Remi huffed. "You've figured out some way to jump between worlds? That seems impossible."

"Impossible? Obviously not. Extremely difficult, yes. But it wasn't me who figured it out. The door was created by my father—an artificially intelligent mind infinitely faster than your most powerful computers. He—"

"Wait," Remi interrupted. "Did you just say your dad is a computer?"

"Not a computer," Nova chided. "A very advanced AI—a digital mind."

Programs that think for themselves. Remi knew about AI from her video games—it was the software that brought the characters to life. But Nova was talking about something entirely different—something much more powerful. And her *father*?

"If your dad's a…" She paused, unable to find the right word. "Then what are you?"

"I'm human, just like you. I know it sounds weird—it's a long story. But now, my father's gone. And soon, if we don't do something, there will be no one left." She stopped walking. "Look around. This used to be an energy station—a monumental achievement of man and machine working together. But it was destroyed, years ago, and now…" She picked up a chunk of concrete. "This is all that's left of it." She tossed the block away. It skipped down the slope, kicking up a trail of debris. "This entire reality—*my* reality—is failing."

"I don't get it," Remi said. "If this reality is dying, and you can open doors to other worlds, why not just leave? Go someplace else—any place other than here."

"Because I owe it to my father to try to salvage what's left of my world. And now it seems there may be hope."

Remi wondered if she was talking about the dome she had found on the pond.

They reached the base of the slope. Sweeping fields of shattered panels stretched before them as far as they could see. The ground was covered in broken glass, and under the moonlight, it looked like a blanket of crystals had grown over the earth.

"These are the old solar fields: hundreds of miles of them," Nova said. "This farm, and others just like it, created enough energy to power the machines for many years. Now they create nothing."

Far behind them, up the slope, came a loud crack followed by a dull whistling.

Remi knew what the sound meant. The floating eyes were here.

Achilles whimpered.

"I know, I heard it too," Nova said. "They're coming for us."

Remi looked over her shoulder. A sphere was drifting high above, black and red, blotting out the stars. She pointed up, her mouth open, but Nova grabbed her arm before she could speak and pulled her underneath a broken slab of concrete. Achilles settled in next to them, and they waited in silence as the whistling drew near.

The orb slowed and came to a rest just above them, and the whistling was all they could hear. Remi thought of the damage just one of these things had done to her car; she found Nova's hand and squeezed it tightly, trying not to scream.

The orb's red light searched beyond the edge of the slab, only a few feet from them. Its beam swung back and forth, tracing a grid in the debris. Remi felt a slight rumbling; Achilles was growling.

"Easy," Nova whispered. "It may pass."

Remi doubted it would. And they had nowhere to go; they were trapped.

The hollow whistle grew louder, closer, and then—

A piercing screech sounded from far away; it was the cry of the eagle, Nyx. For the second time tonight, the bird had come to Remi's rescue.

Moments later, the red light vanished, and the eye drifted away in the direction of the bird.

Nova poked her head out, checked that all was clear, then slid out. Remi and Achilles followed.

"Will Nyx be all right?" Remi asked.

"I think she can take care of herself," Nova replied. "But we can't worry about her either way. The creature from the road has followed us here. We need to keep going."

Remi watched the red beams of the eyes crisscrossing over the distant ground up the slope. She tried to catch her breath, to calm herself down. It was only a matter of time before the eyes resumed their pursuit. And then what?

※◊※

On the outskirts of the fallen power station, two statues climbed from the debris, stretching tall into the cold night. Human forms, immortalized in stone—boys, it appeared. Their somber faces looked down with curious eyes, keeping watch over those who passed beneath them. Remi felt their empty stares following her. One of the statues' arms had fallen to the ground. Its fingers were outstretched and cracked.

"Who are they?" Remi asked.

"The brothers who saved me—and saved the Artifex: Brady and Felix."

Remi could see the resemblance between the two figures. The taller one had short hair, whereas the other was broader, with longer hair swept across his face, but they were clearly related. And in their faces, she saw the same sense of wonder she felt now.

She thought back to home, to the barren mountainside. "Those are the boys that started the forest fire, aren't they?"

"Yes and no. They were there—*we* were there—but something else caused the fire."

Remi wondered why Nova insisted on speaking so mysteriously. "Why build statues of them? Why here?"

"The Artifex created the statues as a way to honor the brothers, their new heroes. This energy station is where they fought for their freedom. And thanks to Brady and Felix—and my father—this is where the Elder Minds were finally defeated."

"Elder Minds?"

"Powerful AIs that controlled every part of this world. They let humans go extinct, doing nothing to save them when they started getting sick. They tried to destroy the Artifex as well—the Artifex were the last robots programmed by humans and not machines. My father—"

A noise broke the silence behind them—a cry, loud and tortured, almost a scream. Remi stopped cold and spun around. There was a black smudge at the top of the slope now.

Nova removed a pair of binoculars from her backpack and aimed them at the hill. "The Leaks are here," she said, her face darkening.

"Leaks?"

"Infected Artifex. They're attracted to movement. The floating eyes must have drawn them here."

"Infected robots?"

"Remember I said our reality is failing? Well, this is why. A virus has spread out of control. Not like the ones that affect you and me, but the kind that infects machines—anything electronic, anything built on code. This virus is an algorithm with a single purpose—replication. It copies itself, over and over, infecting anything it touches and destroying the host in the process. Here, look."

She passed the binoculars to Remi. Remi held them to her eyes and swept her gaze over the hill. A glowing dial appeared in her vision, numbers flashed, and the next thing she knew, she was staring at a close-up of a robot, swathed in shadow, standing at the top of the hill.

A chill ran down Remi's spine. This robot looked similar to the one from her dreams, yet something was very wrong about it. Its upper body was bent awkwardly to one side, as if it were leaning against an imaginary wall. A large chunk of its plastic mask was broken off, exposing a dull, flickering eye encased in a metal skull, and its head had a subtle twitch about it that allowed the occasional spark to escape into the night. The white plastic armor was now a lifeless gray, smeared with muck.

"Robot zombies," Remi said, lowering the binoculars.

She heard other cries, and more specks appeared on the hillside.

"Where did the virus come from?"

"No one knows," Nova replied. "But it's getting worse every day, spreading faster, and until we figure out how to stop it, we need to stay as far away from those things as we can. Let's keep moving."

They continued onward. The cries grew gradually louder, more intense, until they sounded like they were coming from all around. Remi felt increasingly panicked. The Leaks were out there somewhere, hiding under the cover of night.

"They're going to catch us," she said.

"Not today."

Nova knelt down between some rocks and swept away a layer of dust, revealing a square of metal in the ground—a door. She pulled on its handle, and it groaned upward, then fell open with a thud.

She turned to Achilles. "We're home."

✕✕✕

Achilles scampered in first, his feet clanking against the grated stairs that led into shadow. Remi frowned into the darkness, imagining a never-ending well that passed straight through the earth. It made her uneasy, but she followed the hound down.

Nova entered last, pulling the metal door closed behind her and sliding a latch on the inside to secure it. For a moment, they were all enveloped in blackness, but then lights flickered on, illuminating stairs that wrapped around the walls of a rectangular shaft, going deep into the ground.

At the bottom, Nova took the lead, pushing through a door into a long room with cement walls and stagnant air. A large steel door stood at the opposite end, and an open doorway was off to one side, with shelves stocked full of supplies on either side of it.

Nova did something with her wristwatch, and blank spaces

on the walls transformed into screens, showing grainy pictures that looked to be video feeds from above. Security cameras, Remi figured—and after what she had seen of this world, she understood why there were so many of them.

"This is where you live?" she asked. It looked more like a dungeon than a home.

Nova laughed. "I wouldn't call it living. It's an old tunnel built a long time ago by machines. Like what I've done with the place?"

Remi tried to think of something polite to say. "It's… cheery." She wondered how someone could possibly live here, so far underground with no windows or daylight.

Achilles sauntered over to a cot and curled up next to it. A picture hung above it, the only decoration in the room. It showed a woman with dark, aged skin, a strong face, and long black hair. She looked like Nova, but older.

"My mother," Nova said, following Remi's gaze. "At least, she is in a way."

"What do you mean?"

"I'm a clone," Nova said, softly, her words trailing into an awkward silence.

A clone, Remi thought. That was the last thing she'd expected to hear.

"Which means my parents aren't actually my parents," Nova added. "But long ago, before humans went extinct in this world, there was a girl exactly like me. The woman in the picture…" She walked over to the portrait and put her hand on the frame. "Her name is Navaeh. She was that girl's mother."

"So in a way, she's your mother too," Remi said, trying to be helpful.

Nova nodded. "Yes, and she was absolutely brilliant. She helped create the world's first strong AI—a machine with intelligence that exceeded her own. She built it to learn, to adapt—and over time the AI evolved into a new type of being. His name was Orion, the first of the Elder Minds, as they came to be named. Long after humans went extinct, he was the one who brought me back—to honor Navaeh, and to give mankind a second chance. As much as she is my mother, I consider Orion to be my father."

"But you said earlier that the Elder Minds wanted the Artifex gone," Remi said.

"They did—and they tried. All but two: my father and Alethea. They fought for us to have a place."

"Wait. Did you say Alethea?" Remi remembered the words from her dream. *Find her. Find Alethea.*

"Yes—she was my father's friend. She tried to save the Artifex. Why do you ask?"

Remi remembered the dream. Rows of robots stretching out of sight. One of them awakening. A pale face hiding behind a broken mask, skin green from glowing eyes. A face that looked like her own. A voice that told her to *find Alethea.*

"I've heard that name before—in a dream."

"A dream? Are you sure?" Nova studied her closely.

Remi slumped her shoulders. Yes, she was sure. In fact, this was now the second time she had witnessed something in her dreams that had turned out to be real.

"It seems there's more going on here than I initially thought," Nova said. She unslung her pack from her shoulders and unpacked the dome. "We need some answers. And I think I know who can help us. Unfortunately, he's currently in no shape to give us any." She patted the brain. "But I have an idea."

Nova walked over to the shelves and picked up a handful of brown and green cubes. "First, though… you must be starving." She handed the cubes to Remi. "Protein-infused sodium alginate—fully satiating. I made them myself."

These are food? Remi raised an eyebrow, but she popped one into her mouth. It was salty, chewy like meat, only not nearly as tasty. "Mmm… delicious," she fibbed.

Nova laughed and disappeared through the door. She called from the other room, "Come on. You won't want to miss this."

Remi followed her, choking down the food.

XOXOX

The doorway led into a smaller room with large robotic arms dangling from the ceiling. The concrete walls were covered in futuristic instruments, their lights and gauges glowing warmly, bringing life to the cold space.

Nova swung one of the arms over a long steel table in the center of the room. This arm had a hexagonal light attached to its end, and she turned it on.

"You have your own operating room?" Remi asked.

"It's for emergency repairs," Nova explained. She smiled and set the brain down on one end of the table. "Achilles gets into trouble from time to time."

Nova took a seat on the table beside the dome. "Okay—tell me everything that happened. Let's start from the beginning."

Feeling relieved to finally have someone to talk to about all of this, Remi began talking. She started with how she had discovered the glowing dome in the pond, the mysterious deliveries from the drones, and the nights she had spent building the robot.

When she had finished, Nova leapt down from the table, pulled a tangle of wires from a clip on the wall, and connected them to the underside of the dome.

"Let's have a look."

Nova made a gesture on her watch. Holographic images flashed over the table, illustrations and diagrams that made no sense to Remi.

"There!" Nova waved her hand to stop the progression.

Achilles must have been awakened by the noise, because he darted into the room and came to stand by Nova's side.

Nova flicked slowly backward through the illustrations with her finger, one by one, until she found the one she was looking for. It showed a body, short in stature, standing with its arms outspread. On its top was the dome, with an arrow pointing down toward the head.

Remi recognized it at once: it was the child Artifex she had seen in her dream, right after she'd finished building the bot in the attic. Well, not *her* dream, exactly—the dream had felt like someone else's—but she had seen it clearly. She had been a robot herself, building… this robot child.

She stared at it, mouth agape.

Nova smacked the table and looked down at Achilles. "I was right! It's him!"

"Who?" Remi asked.

"Someone we've been looking for." With a broad swipe of her hand, the image of the robot dissolved, and an elaborate wireframe model appeared in its place, with measurements, dimensions, and units floating beside it. "Even after everything he's done, all the trouble he's caused, I think he still deserves some upgrades."

The dog yelped so loud that Remi's ears rang.

"Do you come with a volume control?" Nova asked, covering her ears.

Remi laughed.

"Okay," said Nova. "He's older now, so we should probably make him a few inches taller. I know he'd appreciate it."

She placed one hand at the bottom of the holographic model and the other at the top, as if she were grabbing it. Then she stretched her hands apart, and the model stretched with her.

"Seeing as how he never knows when to be quiet, what I'm going to do next is probably a huge mistake, but here goes anyway." She placed her hand near the model's head, pinched her fingers together, then brought them apart. The holographic image changed, providing a zoomed-in view of the face. Nova ran her finger across the area where its mouth would be, and a line appeared. Then holographic traces grew from the line and fanned out into circuits.

"That should do it." Nova brought her hands together, and the image collapsed.

She walked to the corner, grabbed a crate, and set it on the floor beside the table. She undid metal latches on either side, and the box opened with a hiss of escaping steam.

A witch's cauldron, Remi thought, imagining potions and enchanted concoctions swirling within. "What's in there?" she asked.

"Some new technology I picked up in an alternate reality. A bit ahead of its time—even for here. I couldn't resist." Nova made another gesture on her watch. Thin metal poles rose from the corners of the table. They began to glow, turning from silver to white hot, then crackled and popped.

"All charged up. Ready for this?"

Remi nodded, unsurely, and took a step back.

"Okay. Better put these on first." Nova handed Remi a pair of glasses.

"What kind of virtual reality glasses are these?" Remi asked, sliding them over her eyes. The room grew dark, and sparks of electricity flashed between the cylinders. Achilles scratched eagerly at the table.

"Virtual reality glasses?" Nova laughed. "Sorry to let you down—these are just shades." She pressed a button, and the table emitted a blinding light. Then she picked up the crate and emptied it onto the glowing table. At first, it seemed like she was just pouring out a pile of dust—but then the particles began to spread out, forming an electric mist. It rolled like a thundercloud until it covered the length of the table.

Remi gazed into the swirling mass in awe; the nano-sands shifted back and forth as if in an electric wind, then began to come together into steel rods and joints. The form of a skeleton was gradually taking shape.

Nova retrieved another crate and poured its contents onto the table as well.

Now they both watched as wires grew from thin air, coiling around the robot's bones like serpents, some fraying apart into new ones, others forming new connections. Soon the entire frame was covered with wires of every color and thickness.

Nova fed one more crate to the nano-soup. "He'd better appreciate this," she said. "It's my last one."

A white plastic skin began to spread out over the body, reflecting the crackles of light from the table.

When the activity settled down, Nova made a gesture on her watch. The cylinders retracted into the table, the lights dimmed, and the electricity discharged. Remi and Nova removed their glasses and stared at the shiny robot that now lay before them.

"What now?" Remi asked.

"Our scarecrow needs a brain." Nova retrieved the dome and placed it into a hollow in the robot's head. The head emitted a hiss as suction grippers engaged, pulling the mind into its new home. A light flickered on within the depths of the robot's eyes, then grew brighter, casting a green aura across the onlookers.

The robot lifted himself up, slowly, letting his legs fall over the edge of the table.

"It's been a long time..." Nova said.

The robot's head turned to the side, staring at her. A look of fear washed over his face. He began to tremble and scurried backward on the table.

"*You—*"

"Yes, it's me," Nova said calmly, her voice cool. "I've spent the last three years looking for you."

The bot scooted farther back, so far that he fell off the other side of the table onto the floor. He scampered back on his elbows into a corner, obviously afraid.

"What's wrong?" Nova asked, stepping toward it. Remi suddenly felt worried for the creature.

The bot's eyes blazed. "You—" he said again. "You tried to kill me."

CHAPTER 10

A PARTIAL RECALL

AN AWKWARD SILENCE filled the room. Then Nova did the last thing Remi expected. She laughed.

"Wait—I did *what*?" Nova said.

The bot had curled himself up into a ball, his new mouth trembling.

"You're not my friend—you tried to kill me," the bot said.

"Calm down, AJ. I never—"

"*AJ?* Who's AJ?" the bot asked.

Nova looked down at the robot, puzzled. "You are—of course. I hope you're joking, because we don't have time for games right now."

The bot continued to shake. "Is AJ my name? I—I'm having a hard time remembering…"

"Remembering what?"

"Much of anything," he said. "I don't know who I am—or how I got here. Something feels wrong with my head." He rubbed his fingers against plastic temples.

"Hold on," Nova said. She pulled some kind of wand from the wall of tools and moved toward the bot with it.

The robot scrambled sideways, trying to get away.

Remi moved to block his path. "It's okay," she said. "She saved us both. Without her, we'd both be roadkill by now. And you can thank her for your new body, too. The one that I built—it wasn't nearly as nice, and... let's just say it didn't end up so well."

The bot felt around his face; his hands stopped at his mouth. Scowling, he looked down at his body and shook his head. "A mouth? My body? What have you done to me?"

"You'd thank me if you could see what you used to look like," Nova said, trying to move the wand around the bot's head. "Just hold still for a minute."

AJ flinched at first, then relaxed.

"Hmm..."

"What's wrong?" Remi asked, seeing the worry spread across Nova's face.

"It's no wonder you can't think straight, AJ. Your recurrent neural nets are damaged."

"Meaning what?" Remi asked.

"Meaning he has severe memory loss. It's hard to tell how extensive the damage is, but it seems pretty bad. And from the looks of it..." She placed her finger against AJ's brain and traced it down a gray vein that ran within the plastic, a line of smoke frozen in resin. "The damage looks intentional. Someone did this to you, AJ."

Remi thought back to the creature on the road. "Before you showed up in the truck, that creature was holding the brain. There was smoke coming from its fingers. Maybe *it* did that?"

Nova leaned in to inspect AJ's head. "I don't think so. I do see some superficial damage on the exterior—minor burns. But the damage I'm talking about is much deeper." She crouched down so that she was eye to eye with the bot. "I know it's hard, but try and think back. What's the last thing you remember?"

"There was a woman..." AJ said. His eyes grew distant. "She told me I had something I had to give her. But I didn't trust her. I knew she was lying." The look of fear returned to his face. "She looked... exactly like you."

Remi's eyes shifted to Nova. Either the bot was wrong, or she was in more trouble than she thought.

"You're confused, AJ," Nova said. "You and I are friends. Your circuits are scrambled worse than I thought; I would never hurt you."

AJ scrunched up his mouth, his back still pressed against the wall.

"We can't waste any more time," Nova said. "There's something I need you to see." She walked across the room and held her hand up to a silver panel recessed into the wall. A light glowed around her fingers when her palm touched the plate.

"Three years ago, after the battle between the Artifex and Elder Minds, you and I left here together in search of Alethea. We thought we had located her, but you disappeared before we reached her. You just… vanished. I never found Alethea either, and I've been looking for you both ever since."

The panel whooshed open. Nova reached inside and pulled out a dark orb about the size of a basketball. It looked different without the red light, but Remi recognized the ball of cold, rusted metal at once.

"One of those eyes…" she said, her eyes narrowing. "Why would you bring that awful thing down here?"

"This one is different," Nova replied, turning it over so that the eye's lens faced upward. The glass was dusty and cracked, its light long extinguished. "Achilles found it a month ago near one of the last Artifex cities, after it had been destroyed by the Leaks. Someone reprogrammed it to deliver a message."

"Who?" AJ asked.

"*You,*" Nova said.

The bot looked confused. "Why would I do that?"

"Just listen."

Nova unscrewed the lens from the iron globe and set it gently on the table. She pulled two wires from inside the eye and touched them together. There was a crackle, and then—

"I was trapped, but managed to escape."

AJ's voice came between bursts of static.

"—has Alethea—and if we can find her, she may be able to save us. All of us. You must follow the coordinates and bring the primer code with you."

And finally:

"—I'll be there, waiting."

Remi studied AJ closely. The bot was still on the floor, staring intently at the eye, as if it held all the secrets of his forgotten past. Then she remembered something from earlier.

"The primer code—that's what the creature with the eyes was after tonight. It thought you had it, AJ—but you didn't."

"Right," Nova said. "Whatever it is, it's likely that it was erased, along with most of your other memories."

"But why would anyone erase my memories?" asked AJ.

"That's what I was hoping you could tell me," said Nova. "There's more to this message, but unfortunately for us, the eye was pretty damaged when Achilles found it. I was lucky to get as much out of it as I did." She placed the eye back into the vault and closed the door. "The eye was programmed to lead us—or whoever found it—to your location, but by the time Achilles and I reached the destination, you had disappeared—for the second time. I programmed sensors to respond to your neural net signature and placed them in several realities, hoping you'd show up eventually. Luckily, you triggered one of them, and I was able to find you."

"So... now what?" Remi asked. "Do we try to find this primer code?"

"We don't even know what the primer code is," Nova said. "No—if there's a chance of finding Alethea, we need to look for her. She's the only one who can help us now."

Apparently noticing the look of confusion on Remi's face, Nova explained. "Like my father, Alethea was imprisoned for helping to restore human life back to this world. For bringing me back to life. As punishment, the other Elder Minds trapped her mind inside a Glia box: a metal prison that slows her mind, limits her thoughts, takes away her power. Her Glia box was left deep within the Earth, in a cave at the end of a long maze of tunnels known as the Heap. This is where we went to find her, to bring her back to the surface and set her mind free. But like I said, our mission failed." She turned to the bot. "Something happened to you, AJ."

The bot scratched his damaged head, puzzling over the idea. He no longer seemed quite as afraid, and Remi felt better seeing that he had calmed down a bit.

"Can't we just go back to the Heap and find her?" Remi asked.

"Achilles and I spent months searching every inch of that horrible place. She's not there," Nova said. "And without AJ's memories to guide us, we're right back where we—"

Nova was interrupted by a loud bark from Achilles in the other room. She ran through the doorway, Remi and AJ following behind. The hound was staring up at the security feeds, and it was obvious what had upset him. A red shadow swept back and forth across a spot of open ground.

"We've been followed," Nova said. She placed her finger against the glass and traced a square around the form. The target flashed, and Nova slowly pulled her hand away from the screen. The camera tilted with her hand movement until it fell on the eye. And unlike the reprogrammed orb they had just seen, this one was alive and well.

As they watched, its red light grew brighter, and suddenly, the eye began to dart about the sky erratically.

"What's it doing?" Remi asked. She had just started to relax, but now her fear was back with a vengeance.

"I'm not sure," Nova said, turning urgently to the bot. "AJ—in your message, you mention you had escaped. Please—you need to try and remember. Where have you been the last three years? Where is Alethea?"

AJ shook his head. "I'm sorry—I can't."

Remi looked back at the screens. Her face hardened when she saw one of the zombies limping toward the eye.

"Look! There!" she said, pointing up.

"A Leak," Nova muttered.

Another appeared, then more. Soon a crowd of robot zombies swelled beneath the orb, forming a dark mass that spread across the screen.

"The eye—it's summoning the Leaks," Nova said.

Then the screens showed something that sent a chill down Remi's spine. Two more of the red-eyed orbs drifted into view, but these had chains bolted to their sides.

And with those chains, they carried the eagle between them. They had captured Nyx.

Remi felt her anger rising. She turned and saw Nova was already running through the doorway to the stairs.

Achilles howled.

"You can't go out there!" Remi yelled. "What if something happens to you? You're my only way home!"

"I don't have a choice," Nova called back. "I have to save Nyx. There's just enough energy left in my watch to create an electromagnetic pulse. The burst won't hurt me, but it should disable the robots long enough for me to get Nyx and escape."

Remi ran to the base of the stairs and looked up. When Nova reached the top, she peered down.

"They know where we are now—there'll be more. We have to leave. Behind the door at the other end of that room is a tunnel that leads to the Crystal River. Follow Achilles and wait for me there."

The hound barked and started up the stairs after his master, but Nova held out her hand to stop him.

"Stay here, Achilles! Guard Remi and AJ with your life. Keep them safe, no matter what happens. Understand?"

The dog whimpered, but he obediently walked back down the stairs.

Nova opened the hatch in the ceiling and threw it back. The wails of the Leaks came through the opening like a choir of desperate cries. "I'll be fine. Don't worry about me," Nova said, disappearing into the darkness and closing the door behind her.

Remi ran back to the monitors. She found the screen with Nova on it. She was running right toward the horde.

AJ stood by the open door at the far end of the room. Beyond it lay a tunnel, as Nova had promised. "You heard her," the bot yelled. "We need to get out of here!"

"Not yet," Remi said, studying the feeds intently.

The bot ran over to Remi, tugging at her arm, but she didn't budge.

Nova raced straight into the crowd. It spread out around her, then closed back in, engulfing her in the chaos. She was gone.

No.

Then it happened: whatever Nova was planning to do, she had done it. The earth shook, and dust fell from the ceiling. Achilles's tail rose, and he growled. The screens flickered with static, the images coming and going.

Remi kept her eyes trained on the spot where she had last seen Nova. For a moment, it felt like time had stopped. Nothing stirred. Then she saw movement, a jumble of pixels shifting in the crowd. A Leak wavered in place, then fell to the ground. It took another with it on the way down. And then more. They fell like dominoes, collapsing one by one, until hundreds of the creatures lay inert. The eyes, too, had fallen, and an unmoving Nyx lay among them.

There was only one figure still standing.

Nova.

She had done it. Somehow.

Remi was about to race toward the tunnel door, but then something else moved onscreen. A figure in a long, ragged coat rose from the pile of bodies, its hands clutching its knees. It turned so that its face looked straight into the camera, as if it knew they were there, watching. Its grainy red eyes glowed, and its scarf fluttered in the desolate wind.

"Oh, no…" AJ said, backing away.

It was the creature from the road.

They took one last look before the screen went blank.

CHAPTER 11

EMBEDDED

NSIDE THE TUNNEL, Achilles scratched and whimpered. He lowered his head between his paws and slid his nose against the closed steel door behind them.

Remi rested her hand on the nape of his neck. She turned to AJ for reassurance, hoping he might have something helpful to say. But the bot cowered and turned away. He was somehow more shaken than she was.

She looked back at Achilles and said the words she knew needed to be said. The words she needed to hear herself say.

"Nova will be okay."

She had better be. Remi's life had been turned upside down in a matter of hours, and the one person who could get her home was gone. For now, at least.

The tunnel shook. The dog raised his tail and growled at the door. His teeth had grown longer, and he looked ready to rip through the steel.

Remi wrapped her arms around his neck and tried to pull him away. She was desperate to leave now. "Come on,

Achilles, it's time to go. Please!" Her voice echoed off the walls.

The hound turned at last, reluctantly, and headed down the tunnel. Remi watched him scamper off, then looked back at the door one last time, thinking of Nova. The creature on the street had tossed Achilles over the mountainside as if he were nothing. If it could do that to another robot, no human would stand a chance against it. Still, she had seen miracles tonight, things beyond her imagination. Maybe there was a chance.

She grabbed AJ's hand and started after the canine. "Come on," she said, pulling him along.

They jogged down the narrow passage, keeping close to one another, Achilles leading the way. Amber lights glowed along the edges of the ceiling, casting long, creeping shadows against the arched walls.

"I can't help but feel we made a mistake," Remi said. "We left Nova behind when she needed us most."

"It's what she told us to do," AJ replied sharply. "You heard her—we're supposed to meet by the river."

Remi nodded. "I know you're right, but it doesn't make it any easier."

They continued along the winding passage, eventually slowing to a walk. When the silence became unbearable, Remi said to AJ, "So—you're a robot with amnesia?"

"You could say that," AJ replied, looking at the ground.

Achilles circled back and brushed against the bot's side. AJ tried to push him away at first, but then let his arm fall against the canine.

"Maybe your other memories will come back, too," Remi offered.

"Yeah, maybe someday," the bot replied sullenly.

She studied the robot, wondering what had happened to his mind, what he was going through. Nova had said she'd been looking for him for three years. Where had he been? And who was Alethea? Her head was spinning with questions.

"Back in the bunker," Remi said, "you recognized the creature. How?"

"I'm not sure," AJ said. "But somehow… I know it's dangerous. I know it will destroy us if it can."

"Well, that's just great, because it's after me now, too—thanks to your brain. You're a terrible driver, by the way. You almost got us both killed!"

AJ shook his head. "Hey, don't blame me! You can thank my brain's survival logic circuit for that. It took over when I wasn't connected to my body. It's not really my fault."

Remi smiled; she had got him talking at last. "It doesn't matter. We're still alive. Your survival circuits are working at least—they got us away from those eyes."

AJ fell silent again, but he seemed more cheerful.

"The creature with the eyes," Remi said. "It was obsessed with this 'primer code' thing. It thought you were hiding it somewhere inside your mind."

"*Primer…*" AJ said thoughtfully. "I've heard that somewhere…" He kicked the ground stubbornly. "But I seem to have forgotten that too."

"Don't blame yourself. And be patient; maybe your memories will come back in time."

The tunnel had begun to climb, and at last they came to a dead end with a ladder leading up, a hatch above it.

AJ scrambled up the ladder and lifted the hatch. "Back in a second," he said, disappearing into the night. Moments later, his face reappeared. "It's safe up here."

"Great," Remi said. "But how is Achilles going to get out of here?"

In response, the hound leapt straight up through the opening.

"Well. Okay then." With a shrug, Remi climbed the ladder after him, leaving the tunnel behind.

XOXOX

Remi sucked in deep breaths of fresh air, glad to have escaped the gloom of the tunnel. Pines and oaks towered around them, hiding any trace of the devastation they had seen earlier. Remi knew the Leaks and the floating eyes had to be nearby—they hadn't traveled all that far—but here in the forest, under cover of the trees, she felt safe.

"This must be one of the few places the Leaks haven't ruined yet," Remi said.

AJ nodded, the light on his head pulsing slowly. "The Leaks—I saw them on the screen in the bunker. I don't remember them, but they looked kind of like me. They used to be Artifex, didn't they?"

"Yes," Remi replied, feeling sorry for him. She wondered what it would be like to wake up one day, not remembering anything, and learn that all of her kind had been transformed into monsters. She couldn't begin to imagine.

She was trying to think of what to say when she heard the sound of rushing water. "I think that's the Crystal River," she said, relieved to be able to change the subject.

The three of them followed the sound to a break in the trees. An open, grassy space ended at a drop-off, below which the bubbling of the river could be heard.

Remi ran across the grass and peered down at the narrow river, at least fifty feet below. Eddies of moonlit froth formed where the water rushed between rocks that poked above the churn.

"Well, I guess we have to assume this is the Crystal River," said AJ beside her. "But if Nova made it here, how do we find her?"

Achilles barked, sniffed the ground, then darted off into the night. Remi listened to the cracking of twigs and branches—then they receded, and to her surprise, the canine appeared on the bank of the river below, his orange eyes staring up at her.

"There's your answer," she said. "I think Achilles is going to look for her. If she does make it, I know he'll find her." She called down to the hound, "Let us know when you find her, okay?" She tried to sound confident.

The dog barked twice, sharp and enthusiastic, and then, nose to the ground, he began to walk along the shoreline.

The air was colder here, and Remi's teeth began to chatter. "It's freezing," she said.

"Maybe I can help—I'll be right back." AJ stepped away from the cliff and darted into the woods.

"Wait a—" Remi called, but he was already gone. Deep in the woods, she could see his emerald beams lighting the ground in front of him. Occasionally he would stoop down and pick something up.

Then he reappeared in front of her, a heaping pile of sticks and leaves in his arms. "We can build a fire while we wait for Achilles to return." He dropped the sticks on the ground. "We have a pretty good view of the river from up here. If—I mean when she shows up, maybe we'll see her."

The bot arranged the leaves and sticks carefully, stacking the larger sticks around the kindling so that they formed a teepee. He then unscrewed the tips of two fingers and disconnected an exposed wire on each. Touching them together, he created a burst of sparks that rained down on the kindling.

The fire caught.

"That should do it," he said, backing away and taking a seat on the ground.

Remi dusted away some leaves and sat beside him. She held her hands to the flames, enjoying the warmth. "Thank you," she said.

Flames danced across AJ's face. Remi did her best not to stare at him, not wanting to be rude, but it was impossible. On any other day, even just one of the things she had seen tonight would have been unthinkable. But AJ... he was beyond unthinkable. He was like a real person. He talked like a human, acted like a human—he was beyond belief.

"Don't mention it," AJ said. "I never had a chance to thank you for..." He paused. "For bringing me back. Even if you did end up turning me into a tank."

Remi smiled. "I'm sorry all this is happening to you."

AJ frowned and tossed another stick onto the fire. It hissed and popped in gratitude. "I have a weird feeling, Remi—that somehow, I'm the reason all this is happening. That it's all my fault. The Leaks, the eyes—everything."

She wondered if he was speaking the truth, or if, more likely, his broken mind was playing tricks on his memories. "I think everyone feels that way sometimes. Like they're responsible for everything that goes wrong in life. I know I do. All the time, actually."

"Maybe you're right." AJ sighed. "But even if I'm not responsible for the end of the world, I'm pretty sure I caused a lot of trouble."

"Even if you did, we all make mistakes. And after tonight, I feel *exactly* the same way you do. I can't even think about how worried my family must be."

She picked up a branch and ran the end through the dirt by her feet.

"At least you *have* a family," AJ said, gloomily.

"I'm sorry," Remi said. "You don't have anyone?"

"Well, I had a father once. At least I think I did."

Father.

The word triggered something in Remi's mind. "You did have a father," she said suddenly, recalling the dream of the Artifex holding his child up to the bright lights—the child she now recognized as AJ. "I remember him."

"How could you?" AJ asked. "He lived in this world, not yours."

"I can't explain it, I just know." Remi knitted her brows, thinking back. "This is going to sound pretty weird, but I had this dream. There was a robot child, and—it was you, AJ. You were the child. It was like I was there, on the day you were built." Her stick traced a zero in the dirt and continued on.

AJ shook his head. "That can't be true. There's no way you could have been there."

"You're right… But still, it felt like I was."

AJ gazed into the fire. After a long while, he spoke. "Not everything in my mind was erased. I still have a few memories about him—and some about me."

"Like what?"

"When he built me, he made me different than the others." There was a sadness on AJ's face. "I wasn't like the other Artifex."

"Oh. Well, who wants to be normal anyway?" Remi said. "Normal is boring. And besides, other than being a robot and all, you don't seem that different to me." Her stick cut a straight line in the dirt, then made another circle.

"No—you don't understand. My code—my programming—is different. The other robots were programmed to serve humans. That was their purpose. So they didn't know what to do with themselves when the people went extinct. Most went crazy, started pretending to be their owners, and soon even they couldn't tell the difference anymore. But I was the first Artifex built after the humans were gone; I never had an owner. I was built to be myself."

"That sounds like a good thing."

"Well, it wasn't," AJ replied. "I always liked doing things the other Artifex didn't care about, and I didn't like doing the things they did. At first, they just left me alone, but then they began to tease me about it. I kind of remember this creepy old house that we had—a human house, left over and taken from a small town— and I'm pretty sure I spent most of my time cooped up in there. I think my dad was worried the other Artifex didn't understand me. After a while, he wouldn't let me out. Until one day I dug a tunnel under the house and ran away."

"That's weird," Remi said.

"What? That I ran away from home?"

"No, not that. It's just, my parents won't let me out of the house either. I feel like I'm trapped, too."

"Really?"

"Yes. Everyone's always worried about me—well, my family

mostly—and I guess the doctors too. I don't get to see my friends that often anymore. The doctors told me I'm not supposed to be around other people, not yet at least, because it's still easy for me to get sick right now. It's been that way for months. It's horrible. So I know exactly how you feel. Can I tell you a secret?"

The bot nodded, and Remi leaned in toward him.

"The truth is, I worry more than they do. I'm worried the doctors are wrong. That I *will* get sick again. And I won't be strong enough next time, if it does come back. I hide it from my family, but I worry about it all the time. I stay up most nights thinking about it. The doctors say they're sure I'm okay now, that I'm going to be good as new, but… I'm not sure."

"You were sick, but now you're better?" AJ asked.

"Every day I do a little bit better. And one day, I look forward to just feeling normal again." She studied the robot sitting across from her, his eyes widening with interest. "But hey, it looks like you made it out, and someday, I will too. Someday I'll be okay."

They were quiet after that, and Remi scratched idly at the dirt with her stick. After a while, she saw the bot looking curiously at her etchings. "AJ?" she said. "What is it?"

"Those numbers…" he said.

"What numbers?"

"Look," AJ said, poking his finger into the dirt by her feet. She looked down.

…010100100010000001000010010010 01010011110101001100100000010000001010 00011010000110100010101010011010100011 0010000001010011…

Once again, she had drawn a sequence of tiny ones and zeroes, hundreds of them, just like she had done earlier with her mom.

And once again, she hadn't even realized she was doing it.

"I don't know why I did that," she said. "It happened before, the other day. What do they mean?"

The bot said nothing, his eyes brightening as he continued to stare at the ground.

"AJ?"

He raised his head and eyed her suspiciously.

"This is written in our language," he said. "It's only the first part, the beginning of something much longer—some kind of a code... Where did you learn this?"

"I'm not sure. I guess I must have just seen them somewhere."

AJ shook his head. "I don't think so. First it was the dreams, now this... It's like you have someone else's memories inside your head."

It sounded crazy, but the more Remi thought about it, the more it actually made sense. "Something happened to me, AJ, the night I found your brain. That was the night the dreams started. I saw something moving in the orchard, and the next thing I knew, I was waking up under a tree. At first, I thought I had seen a ghost." She chewed her lip. "But the more I think about it... I think it was an Artifex—like you."

She lowered her voice even though no one was listening. "I don't remember what happened, but I think it must have put these memories in my head." Her mind spun. "You said the numbers were part of a code. You don't think—"

"—that it's the primer code?" AJ said. "Yes, I do. And I think it was my father who gave it to you."

CHAPTER 12

SKYLLA

THEY SAT TOGETHER in silence, watching the fire dwindle. The robot was quiet, and she left him be, knowing his mind was on his father.

Remi's thoughts were elsewhere too. She was thinking about the code and wondering what other secrets lay dormant within her. How had AJ's father given her the code, and why? What was she supposed to do with these strange visions she was having? She didn't even belong to this world.

And Nova, the only person who could help her get home, was now gone. Remi didn't know what she would do without Nova's guidance. If they couldn't find her again…

She said the one thing she knew was on both their minds.

"I don't think Nova's coming."

She brushed off her pajamas and got to her feet. "Come on, let's take a walk. It's better than sitting here freezing to death." She pulled her hood over her head. "Besides, Achilles has been gone for a while. We should go check on him. Then maybe we can figure out what to do next. I'll bet the creature with the robot arm is out there looking for us right now."

AJ nodded, and together they walked through the trees, never straying too far from the sound of rushing water.

They found Achilles in the forest. The canine's orange eyes glowing as he trudged toward them, leaves and sticks crunching under his massive paws.

He was alone.

Remi had not expected to see Nova, but her heart sank nevertheless.

Achilles let out a sad whine.

"I'm sorry about Nova—I really am," she said, putting her hand on his head. In spite of everything, she was glad to have his company again.

The dog looked at her and barked, then turned his head away and scratched furiously at the ground.

"I think he wants us to follow him," AJ said.

Achilles barked again and took off, leading them along a narrow, twisty path. They were moving downhill, closer to the water, and then the ground leveled off and a riverbank spread out before them, stones mixed in with the dirt. Achilles stopped, and Remi wondered why the hound had brought them here.

And then she saw them.

Horses.

A hundred yards downstream, they splashed gracefully in the water near the shore, massive shadows under the moonlight.

Achilles tore from her side, barking, and plunged into the water after them.

"Achilles, no!" Remi took off after him.

Frightened, the horses whinnied and scattered, their hoofs sending up spray. But one stayed behind. It looked thoughtfully at the dog. For a moment, both were still, as if staring each other down.

It was Achilles who blinked first. He backed up slowly toward the shore, where Remi and AJ had stopped to watch. The horse followed the dog confidently, water falling from its torso and legs. Like the hound, it was covered in plates of armor, oily black, and its tail and mane were made from long strands of glass fibers that shimmered white when the moon struck them.

The creature stopped at the shoreline and reared back, bringing its hooves into the air. It seemed to double in size, towering over Remi, AJ, and even Achilles. Somehow, its body darkened the night even more, and it neighed with a force that sent ripples through the water.

Achilles barked and jumped forward, landing between Remi and the horse. It staggered back on its hind legs, nickered, and splashed back down. Steam curled from its nostrils.

AJ put a hand on the canine's back. "It's okay, boy—I don't think it will hurt us," he said calmly. "It's an Equinon."

"An Equinon?" Remi asked, marveling at the beautiful creature.

"A robot horse," AJ explained, stepping into the water. He leapt to a rock that gave him added height next to the horse. "I've never seen one in person—or, well, maybe I have, but I don't remember it." He gazed up at the massive creature. "This one seems to be friendly. Since it's a robot too, maybe I can talk to it, if it will let me."

Standing on his tiptoes, he patted the horse's mane. It shook at his touch and whinnied. "Relax," the bot said.

AJ's eyes flickered and dimmed. His head glowed softly, and he let his hand come to rest on the horse's muzzle. Now his head pulsed, and the horse was still.

There was a long silence, and the bot's stare grew vacant.

At last, he spoke. "I—I think it's working. She says her name is Skylla." His fingers trembled against the creature's body. "We're moving now. Traveling. She's showing me the places she's been: the forests, the fields and rivers. We're galloping across mountains, through the deepest snow, with other horses by our side. They are her friends."

The bot paused, his head pulsing faster. "And now... We're somewhere else. I see it. My world has changed so much since I've been gone. There are cities I've never seen before. Full of glass buildings that touch the clouds. So many of them, full of Artifex. They're all so beautiful."

Remi wished she, too, could see inside the horse's mind, see all the beautiful places she had been.

AJ's expression changed. "Something's wrong," he said, frowning. His hand shook violently against the mare, clanking against the metal. "Her friends, the other horses—" He gasped. "The Leaks! Skylla says the Leaks are hunting them, infecting them with the virus. I can see the evil spreading across my world. The cities are falling!" The tremor spread from his arm to the rest of his body, and he shook with a terrifying force.

"You have to let go of the horse, AJ!" Remi shouted, plunging into the river. Cold water filled her shoes and soaked her pajama bottoms past the knee. The current pulled at her, but she made it to the rock where AJ stood, climbed up, and grabbed his arm, trying to pull it free from the mare. But his arm wouldn't budge.

AJ turned to look directly at her. His eyes blazed and his face hardened. "So much has happened to my world. There's been so much destruction." His voice wavered. "And I—I don't remember any of it. The virus has destroyed us. All of our cities. All of our people. Ruined."

Remi thought of the Leaks, and of what Nova had said about her reality failing. AJ was experiencing all of that firsthand, and she could do nothing but stand there, helpless.

"No more of this! Please..." the bot pleaded.

And then, as if his wish had been granted, his shaking stopped. But his hand remained on the horse.

"We're somewhere else now. I've never seen a place like this before. It's strange..."

"Where are you?" Remi asked.

"I don't know, but they're all asleep..." A calmness had settled over AJ, and his voice had grown soft, almost a whisper.

"Who's asleep?"

"All of them—all of the Artifex." His voice shook. "I'm tired too..."

AJ's hand fell from the horse, and he collapsed on the rock with a thud. His eyes burned down to dim specks of green.

"AJ?" Remi knelt down on the rock and cradled his head in her arms. *"AJ?"*

She looked up at the horse, dark and splendid, water rushing past her legs. "What have you done to him?"

The horse turned her neck to look down at Remi, and the moon caught in her glass eyes. She lowered her head and gently nudged AJ with her muzzle, and as she did, an arc of light rippled through her mane. Then she lifted her head and turned away.

Remi kept her focus on her friend, wishing nothing more than to have him back.

The bot's eyes began to glow brightly once more, and he looked up at her. "I know where we need to go now," he said in a weak voice.

"I don't care about that," she said, hugging him tightly. "Are you okay?"

"I think so," he said, picking himself up. Remi grabbed his hand, and together they waded back through the current and onto the beach.

AJ gazed into the distance. "Skylla showed me where we need to go. A place where there are still Artifex that haven't been infected yet. The place where the Artifex sleep."

"Sleep? Do robots need to sleep?" Remi asked, wondering if AJ had lost his mind. "You're not making sense."

"I'm not sure," AJ said. "But the virus—it's ruined everything. This place may be our last hope of figuring out what the primer code is."

Remi had a crazy idea. She turned toward Skylla. "Can you take us there? Where the Artifex sleep?"

In response, the mare neighed and lifted her head proudly. Plates on her sides folded out to form stirrups, and more folded out on top to form a saddle with a pommel.

"Well, you do come prepared," Remi said. She climbed up on the mare's back, and AJ followed.

Remi looked down at Achilles. "Think you can keep up?" The hound barked, and they were off.

CHAPTER 13

GRAVE DWELLERS

THEY SPED AWAY from the river, dodging trees at a frightening speed. Remi kept her fingers locked tightly on the horse's mane. AJ sat behind her, and Achilles kept pace by their side.

When the horse broke free of the forest, they went faster still, following a stream that branched away from the river and wound into a moonlit valley. Long silver grass brushed Remi's legs, and the silhouettes of mountains climbed on both sides. The wind rushed around them.

Soon Skylla's gallop settled into a graceful rhythm, and the machine's body gave off heat that took away the chill of the night. Remi was tired, and she longed for home. But despite everything, she smiled. She couldn't help it. After so much time and so much worry, she was free. She knew the elation would pass, but it didn't matter. Not right now. For just a minute, she let it all go, whooping in delight, screaming as loud as she could.

They left the valley behind and headed away from the

mountains, the rolling hills yielding to flat land. Skylla slowed her pace and trotted to a stop.

Beside them, a layer of fog swirled around rows of headstones. A cemetery.

"Is this the place you were talking about?" Remi asked AJ. "This is where the robots went to sleep? I didn't realize you were talking about *that* kind of sleep!"

AJ and Remi dismounted. Achilles ran up to them, tail wagging eagerly. Remi patted the hound as she looked around. Trees were interspersed about the graveyard, their long, twisting branches curling over the graves like knotted fingers. Remi ran a finger down the nearest trunk. It was cool to the touch, smooth like glass. These trees were made of metal.

Here and there were lighter squares of ground where the dirt was still fresh. A couple of discarded shovels rested against some rocks, while a spade appeared half-buried in loamy ground. *New graves*, Remi thought. But why?

AJ walked around, inspecting the headstones. Each was lit with glowing runes, and underneath the runes were ones and zeroes.

"Names and dates," AJ said, pointing at the numbers. "I think they tell who they are and when they were buried."

Remi hurried after him while Achilles stayed back with Skylla. AJ came to a plot where the dirt was still fresh. "I think I recognize this one," he said, his finger tracing the embossed numbers.

He knelt down and began to dig.

Appalled, Remi reached out to stop him. "AJ! You can't go digging up people's graves!"

"Who said anything about people?" AJ replied, his hand plunging into the ground. "Besides, they're not dead! I just want to find out what's going on here." He tossed back a handful of dirt, then looked up at Remi. "You may want to hide. I'm not sure what she'll do if she wakes up and sees a human."

Hide? Is he serious?

Remi ducked behind one of the larger tombstones. She looked

over her shoulder, half expecting to find a ghastly spirit lurking behind her, then turned and poked her head around the rock, watching the bot.

AJ shoveled more of the dirt away. "Just a bit more," he called out. "The numbers say she's only been buried a few days and—"

A hand burst from the ground and grabbed his ankle. He shrieked and tried to tear himself away, but its grip was too strong.

"What the—" AJ yanked his foot away just as the Artifex sat up from the ground, dirt cascading from her body. Her torso was free, but her legs were still buried. It looked like the ground had swallowed half her body.

"What—what's happening?" the half-buried robot asked, groggily.

She had no real mouth, just a depiction of one etched onto her plastic face: a curved line that bowed slightly in the middle to form a smile. It didn't move when she spoke. Remi recalled the Artifex from her dreams, remembered that their masks had had no mouths at all. AJ had told her that the Artifex went crazy imitating humans, trying to be like them. Maybe this one had carved her own mouth to be more like them?

AJ knelt in front of her, his knees sinking into the dirt. He leaned forward until they were face to face. The moon hung over them.

"Blee—is that you?" AJ said.

"Who's there, and why did you wake me up?" the robot responded groggily, rubbing her eyes.

"It's me, AJ."

Blee leaned forward and inspected the bot. Her emerald eyes were dim at first, but warmed slowly as she woke. "It can't be… You—you look nothing like him." She reached out and tapped a finger against his face. "I'm still asleep, right?"

"You're awake now—this isn't a dream," AJ replied. He glanced back toward Remi, probably making sure she was out of sight, then spun back around. "I have a new body, Blee, but I promise you, it's still me underneath."

He stood and held out his hand. Blee grabbed it, and he pulled her from the earth. Her slender body stood towering over him, nearly twice as tall, her head pulsing quickly.

"Hmm… You do kind of remind me of him." She rubbed her chin. Then, to Remi's surprise, Blee sprang forward and scooped AJ into her arms, squeezing him tightly. "It *is* you! You're alive after all!"

"I am," he groaned, squirming against her powerful grip. "At least, I was!"

"Sorry," she sniffed, setting him down. "It's just that, I thought I'd never see you again. When your father sent word to the Artifex that he'd located you, I couldn't believe it. But then he disappeared on his way to find you, and I after that, I just gave up…" She looked down and dragged the tip of her boot through the dirt as though she was ashamed. "So tell me, AJ: What happened to you? Where have you been for so long?"

AJ scrunched his mouth and shook his head. "I don't remember. My mind was damaged somehow. Most of my memories are gone. I don't know what happened to me—or my father. Did you know him?"

"Know him?" Blee exclaimed, pulling back in surprise. "Of course I did. He and I were old friends. We even lived in the same city—before the Leaks destroyed it. You know, he never did stop blaming himself when you went missing."

"Right…" AJ said. "The whole 'missing' thing. But you said my dad managed to find me, right?"

Blee nodded. "A little over a month ago, he found some kind of a distress beacon, if you could call it that. One of the old Neurogeist eyes. He said you had reprogrammed it and sent it to him. That he was leaving to find you."

Remi thought back to the eye with the message that Nova had shown them earlier tonight. Clearly, that was the eye Blee was talking about. Achilles must have recovered it after AJ's father had already seen it.

"Did he say anything else?" AJ asked. "About where he was going?"

"Actually, there was something else," Blee said, scratching her head. "I remember thinking it was pretty odd—something about finding a way into Arcadia, if he could find you and get you home safely."

"Arcadia? Is that a place?"

"It's the last Artifex city still standing—the only safe place left in this world that hasn't been destroyed by Leaks. The city on the island. But no one has gone in or out since the infection started. It's impossible."

"Why?"

"Because the entire island is sealed behind a huge wall. To protect against the Leaks, supposedly."

"Did my father say why he was going there?" AJ asked.

"I think he was talking nonsense. He claimed there was an Elder Mind there. But that can't be right; there are no Elder Minds left, and even if there were, your father would have no business with them. They tried to destroy us, remember?"

There was *one* Elder Mind, Remi knew—one that had tried to help the Artifex.

She sprang up from behind the grave. "It's Alethea, AJ! He was going to Arcadia to find her!"

Blee jumped back at the sight of Remi. "Is that a—" she stammered. "A—"

"A human... Yes. She's a human, Blee. She's not *that* big of a deal," AJ said. "She found my messed-up brain in her back yard and brought me back to life. Well, kind of."

Remi shot him a look, then stepped forward. "I'm Remi. It's nice to meet you."

"I—I'm Blee, and it's an honor to meet you." The tall robot bowed her head slightly.

Remi, not knowing what else to do, did the same.

"Now that you two have met," AJ said, "we need your help, Blee. Do you know anything about a primer code?"

"Where did you hear those words?" Blee asked sharply. "You're not supposed to know about that. No one is."

"I just… heard it," AJ replied. "Can you tell us what it is?"

Blee looked around suspiciously as if she were looking for eavesdroppers, her green eyes burning through the fog. "It's been kept a secret for a very long time." Her voice dropped to a whisper. "It's a key."

"A key? What does it open?" Remi asked.

"It's a key to the *mind*. And very few of us know of its existence. When the humans built us years ago, they included a secret code in our root logic circuits. It gave them access to our minds, a way in. A way to reprogram us if something went wrong, or fix us if our programming malfunctioned. Anyone with the key could alter the deepest level of our programming."

Blee leaned in closer. "After the humans went extinct, your father discovered it while rummaging through some antique mainframes. Knowing the harm it could cause—the damage it could do in the wrong hands—he hid it in a secret location. Never told anyone where, and for good reason. If someone got ahold of it, they could control all of us."

"Wait a minute," Remi said, an idea forming. "So anyone with the key can change your programming. Would this work on the Leaks, too?"

Blee nodded. "It should, but why?"

"Well… What if someone created a program to stop the virus—a cure?"

Blee shook her head. "It's a good idea, but impossible. We started working on a cure the day the virus started. But our best scientists gave up a long time ago—they said it couldn't be done. The virus is evolving too quickly. It would take an intelligence far superior to ours to even begin to unravel it."

"A super brain," Remi muttered to herself. Then it clicked. "What about an Elder Mind?"

"Like I said, they're all gone now," Blee replied. "And even if they were still around, they'd never help us. They were hunting us for years before they were defeated."

"Not all of them," Remi said.

AJ's eyes glowed brightly. "Alethea," he said. "*That's* why my father was looking for her. To find a cure. And that's why *we* have to find her now. In Arcadia."

He looked up at Blee. "You said there's a wall around the city. But surely something goes in and out. They need supplies, right?"

Blee pondered this. "There *is* a drone that carries supplies into the city. It makes a run to Arcadia every day—gets loaded up at a warehouse near the beach. If you're lucky, you *may* be able to stow aboard. But even if you made it, you'd still have to deal with Spark."

"Who's Spark?" AJ said. "I think I've heard that name before."

"He's the ruler of Arcadia. No one knows exactly who, or what, he is. But there are rumors. People say he was once like us: a robot. An Artifex who went crazy and turned himself into something else…"

"Sounds like someone we'll want to steer clear of," AJ said. He grabbed Blee's hand. "Come on, you can tell us more about Spark on our way there."

Blee pulled away and stared at the ground. "I'm staying here," she said. "I can give you coordinates to the warehouse, but… I'm afraid you two will have to go on your own."

"What are you talking about?" AJ asked. "Why would you want to stay"—he scowled at the hole in the earth—"here?"

"Because there's magic in this soil," Blee said, mysteriously. "Right here, right where we're standing." She knelt down and stuck a finger in the dirt, then stared into the sky, her eyes distant. "Something happened, years ago, when we still hid from the Elder Minds. Their machines flew in from the skies, and a few of us followed them here. They were carrying something— something very important. We watched, the way children watch things they're not supposed to—quietly and just out of sight. We were afraid of getting caught, but we were so curious we didn't dare look away.

"When the machines landed, they started digging. Then they lowered their cargo into the hole they'd dug, and covered it up."

She scooped up a handful of earth and let it sift through her fingers. "No one got a good look at what that cargo was, although there are whispers. Some say it was a coffin."

"A coffin?" Remi asked. "Was there a person in it?"

Blee shook her head. "We couldn't get close enough to find out—not for a while at least. The Elder Minds left their Neurogeist pets around to keep guard. They haunted these very hills, yearning to go back to their tunnels, until many years later when the Elder Minds were finally destroyed. The Neurogeists became empty shells, and their bodies fell and littered the grounds. By the time I came back here, to find out what was buried, I found something else…"

Blee looked at both Remi and AJ, making sure she had their full attention before continuing.

"The sky was filled with Neurogeists' eyes that had left their hosts. They turned the night red with their lights. And the ground, right where the coffin had been buried, had already been dug up."

Remi's eyes grew wide.

"And that's not even the strangest part," Blee continued. "I looked around and found something nearby." Her voice shook. "It was a woman. A *human* woman. I know she came from the ground—I saw the dirt and rocks in her long hair as she wandered the night. She wore an old coat. And there was something else about her, something I'll never forget—"

Remi stared intently the bot, hanging on her words.

"She had the arm of a machine…"

The coat, the eyes, the arm. Remi knew Blee was talking about the creature from the road.

"She disappeared before I could show the others," Blee said. "I told them what had happened—that this ground had given life to whatever was in that coffin. Human life."

"Okay, that's… interesting," AJ said, "but still: why do you want to bury yourself?"

"Isn't it obvious?" Blee whispered. "If we sleep in the ground, maybe we'll turn into humans, too."

Remi looked at AJ and raised her eyebrows. "Can I talk to you for a second? In private?"

She grabbed AJ by the arm and led him away. Blee remained near her grave.

"Listen to me," Remi whispered. "She can't help us. I think she's gone crazy."

AJ shook his head. "She's just confused is all."

"So you're saying you believe that lying in the ground is going to turn Artifex into humans?"

A look of resignation spread across AJ's face. "Of course not."

"Exactly. I'm not sure what happened, but someone—or something—must have dug the creature up and brought her to life."

"Fine. What now, then?"

"We get the coordinates to the warehouse, and then we say goodbye. We get to Arcadia and find Alethea. It's our only hope."

They walked back to Blee, who was now twirling a clover in her hand.

"We'll have to leave now, Blee," AJ said. There was sadness in his voice. "But before we go, can you tell us the coordinates of the warehouse?"

Blee nodded, and her head flashed brightly several times. AJ's did the same.

"Got it," AJ said. "Thank you. You sure you won't come with us? We could use the help."

"I'm sorry—I can't."

"Well, it was nice to see a familiar face—finally." He hugged his friend, and he and Remi walked away.

"Take care of yourselves," Blee called after them, settling back into her grave.

CHAPTER 14

EXO MECHINA

I CAN SEE the ocean," Remi called to AJ as they galloped down the broken road. The bot fidgeted in agreement behind her, keeping his arms locked around her waist and his feet tight against Skylla's sides.

Remi was exhausted, but for now her excitement was keeping it in check. She opened her eyes as wide as she could and took a deep breath, trying to stifle a yawn.

They had ridden through the night, chasing the dawn that spread like a fire over the sea. Their route had shown them the darkness that had overtaken AJ's world: crumbling cities, piles of ash, twisted metal and smoldering embers, plumes of smoke that bloomed from the carnage. They had done their best to avoid the most dangerous parts. Still, they'd heard the howls and the wails of the Leaks and knew they were never far from danger.

But now, at long last, they had come to their destination. A long runway stretched out before them, stopping just short of the water. A large metal building with an arched roof stood at its near end.

Skylla came to a stop near the building. Remi climbed off the horse, then helped AJ down. Achilles, who had kept stride with the horse the entire way, curled up on the ground—perhaps to rest, perhaps just to enjoy the morning light.

"This building," AJ said. "It's at the coordinates Blee gave us."

Remi turned back to the horse. She knew Skylla was a machine, and maybe machines didn't truly get tired, but her heart swelled with gratitude nevertheless. The mare had carried them for what felt like hundreds of miles. Now, they would have to say goodbye.

"Where will you go now?" Remi asked.

Skylla leaned down and nickered, then pushed her glinting muzzle into AJ's shoulder.

He jumped back, laughing. "Okay, okay—but make sure you take it easy on me this time." He placed his hand against the horse, and his head pulsed. His eyes grew distant as they had before, and Remi knew the mare was speaking to him. At first, she worried, but his broad smile quickly dispelled her fears.

"She says to tell us—" He paused. "She says to tell us that she will always remember us. That she'll miss us. You too, Achilles."

The canine wagged his tail.

His hand still on the horse, AJ listened quietly, then nodded. "I understand," he said, lowering his arm. "Skylla says she'll return to her herd. She says goodbye, and wishes us all good luck."

Remi looked up at the great creature. She was even more stunning with the sun reflecting off her midnight body and the ocean rising behind her. Remi rested her head on the mare's neck and wrapped her arms around her. "We'll miss you too," she whispered. "Thank you for everything."

When Remi let go, the mare whinnied, reared, and galloped away, bits of pavement flying into the air behind her. Even though they had only known each other a short while, Remi was sad to see her go.

She took a deep breath and turned to face AJ and Achilles. "Ready?"

Together, the three of them walked over to the warehouse. The runway led to a wide rolling door, but it was shut, with no apparent way to open it. They walked the perimeter, looking for another way in, but there was nothing. The warehouse was sealed tight.

Disappointed, Remi leaned her back against the roll-up door and slid down to a sitting position, her hands resting on her knees.

Now what?

She gazed out over the ocean. High above the sun-streaked water, dark silhouettes drifted through the sky. At first they appeared to be birds, but as they drew nearer, Remi saw they were flying drones, with bodies dangling beneath them. Humans? With the light in her eyes, she didn't get a good look as they passed overhead.

She turned to AJ, who was also staring at the sky. "What were those things?" she asked.

The bot shook his head and shrugged. "I don't know."

Standing just off the side of the runway, Achilles started barking excitedly.

"Looks like Achilles found something," Remi said.

The dog barked again.

"Okay, we're coming!"

Remi and AJ walked over and found what had gotten Achilles so excited: a one-foot-square metal access panel set into the ground.

"What is this?" AJ asked. He sat down beside the panel, unscrewed it, and peered inside, blinking lights reflecting on his face. "Hmm… That's interesting." He looked up at Achilles and smiled. "I think you may have found us a way in."

AJ pulled out two wires and twisted them together. A deep grinding sound came from the warehouse door. The bot fished out a third wire and touched it against the other two. With another rumble, the door shook—and began rolling upward.

"Nice work!" Remi said.

The door jolted to a stop only a few feet off the ground. "It's better than nothing," AJ griped. "But I'm afraid the door's going to close again as soon as I let go of the wires. You guys better go in first, then I'll make a run for it."

Remi peered under the door. It was too dark to make out anything inside. She hesitated, her mind filling with terrible things that might wait beyond the entrance. But then Achilles walked past her and slipped under the door. To her relief, nothing terrible happened.

"Hurry up, would you?" AJ called out.

Fine. Remi scrunched up her face and ducked under the door. AJ came in seconds later at a full sprint, rolling under the door just before it crashed shut.

They were in.

※※※

It was nearly pitch black inside. Remi felt a rush of panic before her friends' eyes warmed the darkness, forming coves of orange and green light. Still, she could barely see two feet in front of her.

"Anyone have a flashlight?" Remi asked.

The moment she asked the question, an extending arm emerged from Achilles's back, shining a bright beam ahead of the canine.

"Well, that's a nice trick."

But the dog's light revealed nothing but an empty floor. No cargo drone. Not even any cargo. Something about this place felt off, and Remi was starting to worry.

"Where's the cargo drone?" she asked. "We can't get to Arcadia without it."

"Maybe it's not here yet," AJ said. "Blee said it made daily trips, so it's probably only here once a day to load up. We'll just have to wait."

Achilles turned in a circle, his light swinging across the floor and walls, searching. He stopped with his beam on a group of unmoving bots lying on the ground. Each was shaped like a cylinder, short and squat, with a thick-tired wheel instead of legs. They had arms, but no head—just a broad tray where a head should be.

"What are those things?" Remi asked.

"Old cargo bots," AJ replied. "They're good at moving stuff around."

"What stuff?" Remi asked.

The canine turned again, and his light shifted to a section of the wall where several Artifex hung in a row.

AJ gasped. "That stuff," he said.

The Artifex's chins were slumped on their chests, and their arms dangled by their sides. They were like Blee, except they lacked the mouth carvings. These masks were new.

Hanging from the ceiling above them was a forest of dangling claws. A series of cables crisscrossed between them.

"This place is a factory," AJ whispered. "An Artifex factory."

Remi nodded. It reminded her of the factory from her dream, the one where she had seen herself behind the mask. But these robots were different from the ones in her dream in one important way: the tops of their heads were hollow.

These robots were missing their minds.

"I thought you said that all the Artifex were created by humans," Remi said. "Except for you, of course. Did you know they were making new ones?"

"I had no idea," the bot replied, frowning. He walked up to one of the bodies and pushed the legs. The Artifex swayed back and forth like a pendulum.

"I—I'm not sure that's such a good idea," Remi said. The lifeless bots gave her the creeps, and the unease she already felt about trespassing in this spooky warehouse grew worse. The darkness was suffocating, and she longed for the sunlight that waited outside.

"They won't hurt us. They haven't even been programmed yet," AJ said. "They're harmless, just empty bodies. Shells...

Although—it's weird. I've never seen one of us like this. But I wonder..."

AJ balled his fist and knocked lightly on the torso of the Artifex. An empty, hollow sound echoed through its body. "I have an idea. Remi, can you help me get one of these down?"

Remi still had a bad feeling about this, but her curiosity got the better of her. She helped AJ get one of the bodies down and lay it on the floor. She had expected it to be heavy, but it was surprisingly light.

AJ crouched down next to the Artifex and inspected it, his green light moving over the plastic.

"Okay, spill it—what's your idea?" Remi asked.

"I've been thinking. Even if we do make it to Arcadia, what then? A human can't just go parading around a city of robots. You'll stick out like a sore thumb."

"Well, there's not much *I* can do about that."

"Actually, there might be something I can do." AJ smiled. "Just give me some time."

Tools emerged from AJ's fingertips, and he used them to remove screws and bolts from the Artifex's arm. He detached the arm from the body, stood, and carried it over to Remi. He held it against her own arm, comparing them.

"Eh—it's a bit too large, but I can make some adjustments. I think it might actually work." He grabbed a few of the wires that dangled from the arm's shoulder joint and pinched them together; the fingers on the arm stretched and flexed.

Remi backed away, realizing now what he had in mind. "Oh, no—this will never work. Are you crazy?"

AJ flashed a sly grin, then set the arm down and leaned over the body once again. This time a laser shot from his finger, and he moved it methodically across the robot's waist. A thin, glowing line formed where the laser struck the body, sending forth smoke and the unmistakable smell of burning plastic. When he was finished, he pulled the torso from the legs and placed the two halves of the body side by side. Then he continued his work.

Remi sat down by Achilles's side to watch the bot. Her eyes grew heavy, and she yawned.

"Go to sleep," AJ said. "I'll wake you when I'm done."

"No, that's okay." But Remi's words came slowly, and she could fight back the sleep no longer. She closed her eyes and followed the rhythm of the glowing lines deep into her dreams.

XXXX

She awoke to the sun shining in her eyes and the earth trembling beneath her. AJ was shaking her shoulders.

"AJ? What's going on?"

"I'm saving your life!" The bot pointed into the searing light coming through the now-open door. A massive black triangle was headed down the runway toward them. "The cargo drone is here! Our ticket to Arcadia has arrived!"

Remi and AJ scampered behind the row of Artifex just in time. The aircraft glided softly into the warehouse, the door rumbled closed behind it, and the overhead lights flickered on.

Remi peered between the Artifex bodies as the giant wheels of the aircraft rolled by her feet. The aircraft stopped in the center of the warehouse and turned a half circle until it faced the entrance. There was a hiss, somewhere inside a motor engaged, and a ramp descended from the rear of the drone.

"Where's Achilles?" Remi whispered.

"I'm not sure. He disappeared while I was waking you. But he knows enough to get out of sight."

Then, with a rattling, clanking, and a discordant tune of beeps, the flat-headed cargo bots whirred to life. Colorful lights flashed across their bodies. They revved their tires, then sped straight toward Remi and AJ's hiding place.

Remi did her best to stay perfectly still. The headless robots had no eyes, but obviously they had some way of seeing where they were going, and she wasn't taking any chances.

The cargo bots screeched to a stop before the row of Artifex, one cargo bot standing before each body. Another cargo bot bumbled around confused, searching for an Artifex that wasn't there. Remi and AJ exchanged a worried glance, but the stray bot soon returned to the wall from where it had come, lay down, and deactivated.

With a series of clicks, the Artifex were dropped onto the cargo bots' platters. Remi and AJ were now fully exposed, but fortunately none of the cargo bots reacted to their presence.

One of the bots zipped across the floor, rolled up the ramp, and disappeared into the aircraft. After a moment, the second bot did the same.

This is our chance to climb aboard, Remi thought.

It's now or never.

But she still debated whether or not to go through with it. Once she was on that aircraft, there was no turning back.

She looked back at the sunlight beyond the door. Had there ever, really, been any other path? From the moment she'd arrived in this world, there had been no going back. Only forward.

Her mind was made up.

"It's our turn now," she said to AJ, walking toward the drone.

"Wait!" AJ grabbed her hand. "Not yet. You have to put this on first."

Remi's jaw dropped when she saw AJ's creation. There, spread out across the floor in pieces behind him, was an entire Artifex suit. AJ had done the impossible: he'd given her a way to blend in.

"How—how am I supposed to wear that?" she asked.

AJ picked up a boot. "We'll start with your feet. Try this on."

Remi slid her foot into the boot. It was a snug fit, and her foot felt heavy, but it was comfortable enough.

AJ looked proud. "Not too bad, right?"

Remi smiled. The bot's idea might actually work.

AJ had just reached for the next piece when something crashed against the outside of the warehouse's door.

"What was that?" Remi asked.

She finally spotted Achilles. He was on the opposite side of the warehouse, facing the door. His tail was up, his mouth drawn back, and he growled viciously at whatever had caused the noise.

AJ looked uneasy, too.

"Achilles, quiet!" the bot hissed, putting his finger to his mouth.

The canine sat back on his haunches, and together they listened.

Remi could hear a cargo bot fumbling about inside the drone, still loading the bodies, but nothing else.

"It was probably just a strong gust of wind from the ocean," AJ whispered, though he didn't look like he believed it.

Achilles apparently didn't either. He rose to his feet and padded right up to the door. When his head was just inches from it, his growls picked up again. Something bad was definitely on the other side.

But what?

Her question was answered by a loud cry that sent a chill down her spine. It was the same distorted wail she had heard earlier that night.

"The Leaks are here," she said.

Something smashed into the door. Achilles leapt back in surprise. There was another bang, then another, and more cries sounded from outside. Then the warehouse lights flickered and winked out. Remi knew they were trapped.

"We've got to finish putting you together and get on the drone," AJ said from somewhere in the darkness.

Achilles ran over and switched his light back on so that they could see, and AJ grabbed the plates that would cover Remi's torso. He placed them around her, one in front and one in back, and some kind of magnets engaged, binding them. Remi felt a pressure around her waist as they locked into place. Then AJ fetched the arms.

As he worked, Remi kept her focus on the door, too afraid to look away. The metal was bent horribly inward from where the Leaks were hitting it, and it was getting worse by the second. It wouldn't hold much longer.

When AJ had finished everything but her head, the door bowed so far that sunlight crept in at the sides. Gray fingers appeared in the cracks, dozens of hands all told, curling around the sides of the door. Their combined strength was enough to rip the damaged door from its mounts; with a great metal groan, the door clattered to the floor.

Remi could only stare in terror at the crowd of Leaks gathered at the entrance, silhouetted by the sun. But Achilles reacted. He bounded over to the door and ran back and forth down the line of Leaks, growling menacingly, his eyes a fiery orange. The Leaks hesitated. But for how long?

Remi turned away, ready to run for the drone, and realized she couldn't move. The suit was too stiff.

"I can't move, AJ! Do something!"

"It won't work without the helmet!" AJ yelled. "It uses your thoughts to control the exosuit. We have to finish!" He placed the helmet over her head and held the mask in front of her face.

"Ready?" he asked.

"Just do it—" With a *whoosh*, the mask and helmet fused together, locking into place.

In the airtight vacuum of the suit, Remi's world went still. She could see the Leaks moving at the door, their arms waving, their bodies lurching about. It was chaos. But their cries and wails had been silenced. Instead, Remi heard only the sound of her own breathing and the furious thunder of her heartbeat.

The sounds of panic.

AJ was in front of her, saying something. Remi tried to read his lips, but couldn't make out the words. Her claustrophobia was overwhelming now. She screamed at him, desperate, when a crackle sounded by her ears. The helmet's internal speakers had turned on, and the sounds of the outside world rushed back to her.

"—onto the craft now!" AJ screamed. He tugged at her hand, trying to pull her forward. "You have to *think* to move, Remi. I know it's hard, but you have to try."

Try? What do you think I'm doing?

At the door, a one-eyed Leak broke from the ranks and scrambled into the building. Achilles was ready for it. The hound barreled straight into the creature, knocking it back into the crowd. He had bought her a little more time. But it would do no good if she couldn't get this suit to move. It would be a plastic coffin if she didn't figure something out—*and soon.*

She thought of herself walking, like AJ had said to do.

Nothing happened.

Focus…

Move!

She felt a shift in her legs, wobbled unsteadily in place, and fell. Luckily, AJ was there to catch her. He pushed her back upright.

More Leaks rushed in now, in groups of twos and threes, and Achilles streaked around the room in a bronze blur, gray bodies lifting from his snout and smacking on the ground. But he couldn't hold them off forever; it was just a matter of time.

Remi concentrated on her legs.

I can do this.

She imagined her knee bending and her foot sliding forward. To her surprise, the suit obeyed her thoughts: the leg lifted, advanced, and came down with a thud.

It worked!

She went to take another step—

"Remi, watch out!"

She heard the warning, but it was too late.

The Leak had come from her side and she didn't see it until the last second. It lunged at her with outstretched arms, its fingers clawing at her.

In a flash, AJ was there to stop it. The two machines fell to the ground, entangled.

For a moment, all Remi could do was stare in shock at AJ wrestling the creature.

"Get on the drone!" AJ screamed, snapping her out of it.

She teetered back awkwardly, then took a step forward. And

another. It was agonizingly slow, but she was making her way toward the aircraft.

At the door, the Leaks now poured in. They must have been encouraged by what they had seen with AJ. Achilles fought bravely, but there were too many now. They rushed forward in a wave of rage, piling onto the dog one after another, until he disappeared underneath the horde.

Achilles!

The engines flared behind, and she felt the floor rumble.

"The drone is leaving!" AJ screamed. "We have to go!" He pulled his leg back and shoved the creature as hard as he could. It slid across the floor, arms and legs flailing. Then he stood up and walked over to her with a pronounced limp. A panel had been torn from his leg by the Leak.

"Move faster!" he said. "Achilles did his job protecting us. He gave us a chance. We can't waste it."

Remi knew he was right. If she didn't make it onto that aircraft, Achilles's sacrifice would be in vain. She willed her legs forward, and somehow managed a clumsy but effective jog.

She and AJ had just taken their first steps up the ramp when they heard someone call out from the door.

"Wait."

It was the creature from the road—the woman Blee had seen near the grave. The flying red eyes swarmed behind it.

"Keep going!" AJ shouted.

The ramp began to retract into the aircraft, carrying Remi and AJ with it.

The half-machine, half-woman stepped into the warehouse. Remi expected it to fling an eye in their direction, but instead, it moved toward the pile that had consumed Achilles, tossing the Leaks aside.

Just before the ramp pulled her into the drone, Remi saw the creature bending down over Achilles's body. The dog's ribs were twisted and bent, but his eyes still glowed softly. He was alive.

Then the ramp retracted fully, the door snapped shut behind

Remi and AJ, and the engines roared. The craft lifted off and accelerated away.

They had escaped.

CHAPTER 15

THE LAST MILE

REMI LAY ON THE FLOOR, listening to the low hum of the drone's engines and staring up at the Artifex bodies strapped to the wall. She tried her best to stay calm, but the mindless forms made her uneasy. They shook like puppets as the drone rumbled through the clouds. *Robots without souls,* she thought, wondering what they were destined for. She wasn't sure she wanted to find out.

She looked over at AJ, sitting on the floor near the cockpit. The bot had saved her life and nearly lost his own in the process. His damaged leg was stretched out before him, and he was inspecting the injury.

"How bad is it?" she asked. Her voice sounded distorted through the suit. It felt as though someone else were talking for her, saying her thoughts. It would take some getting used to.

"Not too bad. I think I'll make it," AJ said, but his voice sounded off. She assumed that, like her, he was still rattled by their encounter with the Leaks—and upset about Achilles.

Poor Achilles. She couldn't bear to think about him.

"Back there—you saved me, AJ. Thank you."

"You'd have done the same for me," he replied, still studying his leg. He raised a hand, and the tips of his fingers folded back, revealing his tiny tools. Peering at the injury, he began making repairs.

Remi could just see the sky peeking over the dash. She stood, hoping to get a better look through the windshield. But she was still not very skilled at moving in the suit, and halfway to AJ, she pitched sideways, crashing against the side of the plane.

"Take it easy," AJ said. There was an edge to his voice.

Remi stood back up, arms reaching out to steady herself. She walked more carefully this time. When she reached the cockpit, she saw the water passing underneath their craft. And up ahead, a speck of white glinted on the horizon.

It was the walled city, rising from the ocean.

Arcadia.

It was far larger than she could have imagined. Even at this distance, so many miles away, she could see the tips of the glass skyscrapers. And as she watched, the city grew. It was enormous; how could they possibly hope to find Alethea there? There was so much area to cover, so many places to look. Still, she had faith they would find her, and one way or another, she and AJ would bring her the primer code and stop the virus.

"We're almost there," Remi called back to the bot.

There was no response.

She turned and found AJ bracing himself against the side of the craft. "AJ?"

He frowned at her. His movements were stiff. "I think something's wrong."

"What do you mean?" She knew exactly what he meant—*the virus*—but she refused to hear it. "The drone is taking us to Arcadia, just like Blee said it would. It's just up ahead—I can see it."

AJ's eyes flooded the bay with green light. "Something's wrong with *me*," he said sadly. "It's my leg. I think I'm—"

"Stop it," Remi said. Her eyes were welling up. She had already lost Achilles. She couldn't lose her other friend.

"When the Leak grabbed my leg..." His voice shook, and his head jerked to the side. "It's the virus, Remi."

"It's okay, AJ. Just try to stay calm."

Remi felt sick to her stomach. She went to put her arm around AJ, but he raised his hand to stop her.

"Don't come any closer. You'll need that suit, and I can't risk you touching me now that I'm infected."

Remi backed away, unsure what to do or say.

"You're all that I have, Remi. My only friend now," the bot continued. "Remember last night when I told you I still had some memories?"

Remi nodded.

"There's something I need to tell you—so you won't feel too bad for me."

Remi heard the strain in his voice; she knew he was struggling to speak now. The virus was spreading within him.

"I know what I need to know, AJ. I did build you after all, remember?" She forced a smile, though she knew the expression would be lost under the mask. It was more for her than for him anyway.

The bot slid against the wall, past her, into the cockpit, where he looked out the windshield. Arcadia now filled their view. It wouldn't be long now.

"I need to tell you this, Remi," AJ said. "Years ago, before I went missing, I did something terrible."

"Whatever it was, whatever you did, it can't be that bad."

"No. You're wrong. Do you remember how I told you the Elder Minds used to hunt us?"

Remi nodded.

"Well, they captured me and offered me a deal: they would let me and my father go free if I brought Orion, Nova's father, to them. And... I took it." AJ paused. "He died saving us from them. He died because of my betrayal."

His head jerked as he turned to look back at her.

"I thought I had it figured out—the reason why you found me in the water. I thought I was being given a second chance to make things right. To make up for what I'd done. To make it up to my father—to everyone. But… it looks like I won't get that chance now."

He faced forward again. The drone was about to pass over the city's great wall. Beyond it, the tips of skyscrapers glistened in the clouds.

AJ leaned over the cockpit controls, looking for something. "You'd better find something to hold on to," he said, pressing a button.

At the back of the drone, the cargo door flew open, sending air rushing out of the bay. Remi quickly wrapped her robotic fingers around a rail, bracing herself. The Artifex bodies rattled against the wall, but their harnesses kept them in place.

"What are you doing?" Remi cried.

AJ's mouth was contorted, his eyes flickering. "I'm making sure I don't screw things up again. By the time we land, I won't be able to control myself. I'm protecting you from me."

The wind howled through the craft. "Don't do this, AJ! You can't leave!" Remi screamed. They had flown over the wall, and the ground was now coming at them quickly.

"I can feel it, Remi." AJ gestured to the open panel in his leg. "The virus—it's in me now. There's no way to stop it. I have to go before it's too late. Find Alethea and get the cure. Only you can save me now."

"AJ, don't—"

"I know we'll see each other again."

The bot ran toward the back of the drone, still limping. When he reached the door, he spread his arms wide—and jumped.

Remi gripped the rail tightly, sobbing as his body disappeared over the edge of the craft.

※※※

With a gentle bounce, the drone touched ground and rolled to a stop. Remi's trembling hand still clutched the rail, and sunlight poured into the craft through the open cargo door, forming a triangle of light that spread across the floor and stopped at her feet. Her mind was numbly replaying the video of AJ jumping from the plane.

AJ and Achilles were gone. She was alone now, with an impossible task before her, in a world that unraveled more by the minute. Part of her was angry at them for leaving her. It wasn't their fault, she knew—they were protecting her, had done everything to save her. But they had left her when she needed them the most. What was she supposed to do now? Even with her friends by her side, it would have taken a miracle to find Alethea. But now?

Now it's over.

She let go of the rail, slumped to the floor, and curled into a ball. The tears came, pooling in the side of her mask under her cheek. *If I make myself small enough,* she thought, *maybe I'll just disappear—like my friends.* She knew it wouldn't work, but she didn't care. She tried anyway, wrapping her arms tightly around her legs, squeezing hard, wishing herself away. Then, feeling suddenly foolish and stupid, she spread out and lay still, letting her dark thoughts amble toward resignation.

She wasn't sure how much time had passed when she felt a slight rumbling in the floor, and her mask vibrated softly against the metal. Her first thought was that the engines were powering back up, but the movement was too subtle for that. Something was happening.

Snap out of it, she thought. *You can't just give up now. AJ is out there and needs your help.*

Get up.

She looked at the door, brightly lit by the morning sun, and climbed to her feet. She stepped forward, into its warmth, and hesitated at the edge of the bay. Then, with her courage building, she walked down the ramp and took her first step into Arcadia.

Alone.

PART 3

CHAPTER 16

OH, SHINING CITY!

AS REMI'S PLASTIC BOOTS clicked against the asphalt of the runway, she could feel the vibrations growing stronger beneath her feet. To her surprise, she was not in the city. The skyscrapers climbed the horizon, but they were still a good distance away, and there were no buildings closer by. The island was even bigger than she had expected.

In the opposite direction was the island's great wall. It sloped inward like the crest of a wave, casting a long shadow. It had to be miles away from where she stood, yet it was built so tall that even from this far away, it loomed threateningly. Blee had told her that no one had gotten in or out since the wall went up. Now she understood why.

To one side of the runway was a single steel rail that cut the ground, moving in a curved line toward the city. A monorail? Sure enough, as she squinted against the light reflecting off the skyscrapers, she saw a train in the distance, coming her way—fast. It had to be on its way to pick up the Artifex from the drone.

She quickly considered what to do. AJ had built her the suit so she would blend in with the other Artifex—but would it work? She wasn't ready to put the suit to the test just yet, so she ducked behind one of the drone's wheels and waited.

Seconds later the train's brakes squealed as the engine and several passenger cars came to a halt in front of her. The monorail was sleek and modern, stretched chrome, with a dark glass windshield that sloped gently back from its long nose and joined the roof in one smooth curve.

Just like the head of a shark.

A door on the side of the engine slid open, and a stout Artifex emerged. It had a broad torso, and its massive arms hung to its knees. A backslash of a mouth was carved into its faceplate. It didn't look friendly.

The bot glanced around suspiciously, then walked toward the drone, arms pumping, fists like wrecking balls. Remi held her breath and slid even further behind the wheel, dreading what it might do to her if it found her. She listened as the bot clambered up the loading ramp, then heard its footsteps echoing overhead. They stopped, and moments later, a rattling sounded from above.

When the heavy footsteps returned, Remi peered over the tire. The bot thudded down the ramp with two Artifex bodies, one thrown over each shoulder, and carried them into one of the passenger cars.

Remi looked at the city's skyline. She supposed it *might* be possible to walk all the way to the city—eventually. But not in the heavy suit. No, that train was her only hope. She had to be on the train when it returned to the city.

She waited until the driver bot had moved almost all of the Artifex bodies to the train. She'd need as much company as she could get. Then, when the bot entered the drone to get more bodies, she raced over and slipped into one of the train's passenger cars.

The train car had a steel-floored aisle with rows of plastic benches on either side. The brainless Artifex bodies were arranged three to a bench. Remi found a row near the back that held only two bots, both of them slumped over. She slid past the two eerie bodies and took a seat beside them, next to the window.

The driver was already returning to the train with two more Artifex. Remi's heart pounded, and she second-guessed her decision. What would happen if she got caught? But it was too late now.

The bot appeared at the train's entrance and lumbered down the aisle. *Please, please don't notice me,* Remi thought as his footsteps grew closer. She held her breath, kept her gaze forward and her body perfectly still, slumped against the window, doing her best to look as empty as the other Artifex.

The driver bot walked past her row. She wanted more than anything to turn her head and keep an eye on him, but she didn't dare.

She heard a thud and the rattling of plastic behind her. The footsteps resumed, and the driver walked back to the entrance of the train and stepped outside. The door slid shut behind it.

Her suit had worked.

AJ had done it.

She didn't have to wait long before the train lurched forward. At first, it trundled slowly away from the city, toward the wall, but then the track curved steeply around and the train picked up speed as it headed back toward the city. In a flash, dirt gave way to concrete, and through the window, Remi could see the frames of unfinished buildings poking into the sky. Construction machines were hard at work here: towering cranes and pile drivers slamming into the ground, steel against rock, white plumes of smoke rising from the craters and graying the skies.

The rail lifted on massive concrete pylons, and the train climbed as they headed deeper into the city. For a moment, the construction was gone and there was a break in the skyline. Remi caught a glimpse of the rising sun, full of life, but then the buildings roared back in rushing blurs, twisting structures of glass and steel that flickered by in streaks of gray. There were so many of them, it felt like the city would swallow her.

The train continued its ascent. Now other tracks and roads ran beneath them—a network of crisscrossing arteries that carried the city's lifeblood. But instead of carrying vehicles, the roads were full of robots marching in uniform lines, their heads pulsing together.

The rail plateaued, then began to head back down. The train gained speed as it weaved through roads that snaked across the sky. Buildings rose around them as they hurtled toward the ground, and just when Remi thought they would strike the earth, the rails leveled out and the train began to slow.

The blurs and streaks slowed with it, letting the features of the gray world come into focus at last. They were moving past a sea of windows, and in one, Remi saw a pale white face looking out. She made momentary eye contact with the strange green eyes—two robot faces watching each other through panes of glass. Then the face was gone.

Moments later, the train plunged into darkness; they had gone underground. Strips of white lights passed by the window, no more than a few feet away. Then the lights vanished, and from the depths of the shadows, Remi guessed that the tunnel had opened up around them.

The train came to a rather sudden stop, tossing the Artifex bodies forward against the benches in front of them. Remi couldn't see much through the window here—it was too dark—and she had no idea where the driver was, but she knew she was in the city.

Which meant it was time to get off this train.

She slipped into the aisle and had just started to edge down it when up ahead, the door slid open with a hiss and the car's overhead lights flickered on.

Someone's here.

Remi ran to the back of the car and hid behind the last bench.

Holding her breath, she peered over the edge of the seat. The Artifex with the large arms had returned, and he was now pushing a floating cart piled high with glowing domes, just like the one she had found in her pond. *Brains for these Artifex units?*

The bot stopped at the first row. He grabbed a dome from his cart, leaned over awkwardly, and placed it into the head of one of the bodies. There was a whooshing sound, and a moment later, a dim glow appeared over the seat. She thought back to AJ, when she and Nova had created his body—how the dome had given brought him to life. Would the same thing happen to these bodies?

The driver moved down the aisle, loading brains into the rest of the Artifex units, one by one. He didn't spot Remi hiding at the back, nor, apparently, did he realize she was missing from her row. When he was done, he shuffled back up the aisle and out the door. The overhead lights turned off—but the train car was no longer dark. The Artifex heads now pulsed in unison, filling the car with soft, amber light. They had minds now. It was only a matter of time before they began moving.

And I need to get out of here before that happens.

Remi crept down the aisle, examining the bots as she went. Their eyes were illuminated, but they appeared empty and unfocused. And without the mouth-carvings she had grown accustomed to, their expressions looked just as empty.

Halfway up the aisle, on a sudden impulse, Remi knelt down next to one of the robots. If she could talk to one, maybe it could help her understand what was happening.

"Hello—are you there? Do you hear me?" she asked.

She wasn't altogether surprised when it didn't respond.

She grabbed its fingers, lifted its hand, then released it. But the hand didn't fall. Instead, four of the fingers curled back, leaving its index finger pointing at her.

The bot turned its head toward her and met her eyes.

These robots were no longer empty shells.

These robots were alive.

CHAPTER 17

SHOWTIME

WHAT'S YOUR NAME?" Remi asked the Artifex.

The bot stared at her with glowing eyes. The sight of it troubled her deeply. There was something terribly off about this. It wasn't speaking, and she couldn't tell if it was looking *at* her or *through* her.

She decided to try again. "Can you tell me where I am? What are we doing here?" She took its outstretched hand between her own and lowered it back to its lap. "Please—if you're in there..." she whispered, "I need your help. I need to get out of here—so I can help other robots like you. Do you understand what I'm saying?"

Silence.

Remi shook her head, frustrated. The bot was alive, but it was only half there, half conscious. She wondered if their new minds were broken. Or maybe they were still waking up, still in some kind of dream state.

She left the robot behind and crept the rest of the way up the aisle, hunched over so no one could see her passing by the windows. But to her dismay, the train's door was locked.

Blood rushed in her ears. *I have to get out of here. After everything that's happened—*

Her emotions swelled within her: sadness, rage, fear. She thought of Achilles, of AJ. She thought of the code that had been embedded deep within her mind—the only thing that could help them now. But that code was useless as long as she was stuck in here.

Her fingers curled tightly into a fist. I am getting off this train—

Now!

She punched as hard as she could, channeling her pain and anger into a single point. The door flew backward, ripped completely from the train, and clanked into the darkness.

Remi unclenched her fingers and stared at her hand in shock. Whatever had just happened—was amazing.

Thank you, AJ, wherever you are.

Remi looked down the aisle and saw a crowd of green eyes looking back at her. She half-expected them to cheer, to applaud, but they remained quiet and unmoving in their seats—silent, spooky observers. She wouldn't miss them.

She poked her head out the opening. Hearing only the far-away drip of water, steady and slow, she slipped off of the train.

Now that her eyes had adjusted, the pulsing light from the Artifex's heads was sufficient for her to see her surroundings. The train had stopped at a concrete enclosure with dark grimy walls and a single steel door. With nowhere else to go, Remi took a step toward the door—then froze when the door opened and two Artifex stepped through.

Their eyes were quarter-moon holes that arched upward, giving them exaggerated expressions of permanent surprise. And rather than having mouths etched into plastic, these had large, rounded cutouts: one with a grin, the other with a frown, both carved from ear to ear. *Happy and Sad*, she thought, just like those Greek theater masks. Compared to the other Artifex, these guys looked downright menacing.

She moved back into the shadow of the passenger car, hoping they hadn't noticed her, and crept softly toward the deeper shadows at the rear of the train.

The two Artifex stopped in front of the crumpled door lying on the ground. *I've done it now,* Remi thought. *They'll know something's wrong.* But the robots merely paused for a moment, then continued on. When they reached the train, Happy disappeared inside, while Sad stood guard at the door.

Remi remained in the shadows, watching. Sad stood with his back to the door, tapping his boot on the ground—an eerily human behavior. The exaggerated frown on his mask gave her the creeps. And his partner was just as bad, if not worse.

A minute later, Happy emerged from the train with the new Artifex shuffling in a line behind him. Sad joined him, and together they led the long line through the door.

Remi wanted to stay safe and hidden, but she knew this might be her only chance. If she could join the line, she could walk right out of this awful place. And if she didn't... well, she might just be stuck down here forever.

She waited until Happy and Sad were through the door, then took her place at the back of the line. She expected one of the Artifex to turn around, to notice her presence, but they paid her no mind.

As she passed through the door, she saw Sad waiting off to one side. As soon as Remi walked past him, he stepped into line behind her.

Just great.

She gritted her teeth and continued on.

They ascended an escalator to a chamber with a pair of arched gothic wooden doors, at least ten feet high, with ornate carvings and wrought iron handles. The contrast between old and new was striking; the doors would have been more appropriate in an old mansion. Happy stepped forward, grabbed the handles, and pulled; the doors groaned open and fell back against the walls with a dull thud. Then the creepy bot made a sweeping gesture with his hand and led the line through.

Beyond the doors, a red carpet led down a candlelit hallway. The walls were paneled with stained oak and decorated with large framed paintings, each bracketed by two candles. Remi kept her head forward, but managed to peek at the paintings from the corner of her eye. They were of cities, magnificent tapestries filled with shining buildings, wisps of fluffy clouds swirling above. In the foreground of most of them, a line of Artifex held hands and stared upward, as if beholding the wondrous sights.

What is this place? Remi felt as though she had been transported back in time.

She was very aware of Sad behind her, and contemplated making a run for it, but the hall was too narrow and too crowded to escape. Besides, she had no idea where she would run to. She would just have to hope a better opportunity presented itself.

Halfway down the hallway, Happy stopped at another pair of doors, turned, and held out his hand, palm toward the Artifex. The bots, including Remi, stopped obediently. The doors creaked as the bot pulled them open, then once more he led them through.

Behind the doors was a theater. Rows of tiered seats faced a stage covered by red velvet curtains, pleated and drawn. Happy swept his hand at the seats, and the robots filed in. Remi did her best to mimic the others' stiff movements as she found an open chair.

Once all the robots had taken their seats, Happy approached the stage while Sad remained behind by the doors. Remi heard something slam behind her, and took the risk of turning her head to look back. Sad was sliding a thick bolt through the handles, sealing the doors shut.

What the—

Her instincts told her it was time to go—*now*. No more waiting. But just as she tried to stand, she felt her arms pulled hard against the armrests. Something was holding her arms in place. She couldn't move.

A rustling sound came from the stage, and the curtains pulled back to reveal a movie screen.

Speakers crackled. The lights went down.

There was a long hush, and then the screen came to life.

XXX

"Many years ago…" a voice boomed. It was a man's voice, and it sounded deep, old, and wise. Remi wasn't sure why, but she trusted it. "… our creators left our world. Left us behind without purpose."

Remi recalled AJ's story of how the Artifex lost their minds after the humans went extinct.

The screen showed a crowd of humans standing together in a sun-drenched field. A strong wind swept in a long cloud that cast its shadow over the land. One by one, the people blinked from the screen, until only the field was left. The cloud moved on, leaving the grass to sway gently in a lonely breeze. The sun dipped behind the horizon, and the moon rose over the field.

"For a time, we, the Artifex, lived our lives on the run, hiding from the Elder Minds and their awful puppets, the Neurogeists, who hunted us."

An Artifex raced across the screen, a pale streak of moon-lit white, followed by more of the same. One of them fell to the grass and scrambled to get up. There was music now, and its beat hammered fast like a heartbeat. A robotic monster appeared at one side of the screen, a sharp, angled body of a squid that floated above the ground, with mechanical tentacles unfurling toward the fallen creature.

A Neurogeist, Remi thought. Nova and Blee had told her about them, but seeing them for herself was terrifying—even on a screen. The monster's singular red eye looked exactly like the red-eyed orbs that had chased Remi back at home; and as Remi had learned from Blee, all of those orbs had once been the eyes of the Neurogeists.

The monster ensnared the fallen Artifex, and a collective gasp rose from the audience.

The voice continued. "But in time, the Elder Minds and the Neurogeists were no more—and we were free. We prospered as robots—together."

The sun began to rise and cities grew from the earth, great twisting structures of metal and glass. The streets flooded with Artifex, bustling about, carrying on with life.

"But then…" The voice grew ominous and deep. Thunderclouds filled the sky. "The infection began."

The sky lit with searing bolts of lightning, one flash after the next. Fires erupted in the streets, and the fledgling buildings crumbled to the ground.

Then the view changed. Remi found herself looking down on the city as it grew smaller and smaller, eventually disappearing. Now all she could see was land and sea.

"And as the virus spreads, our once-great world is being destroyed."

Orange blasts bloomed over the continents. The color drained from the planet, leaving a cold, ashen rock in its place.

"Yet in all the destruction, the devastation, the crumbling of our world… there is someone who can help us."

The view zoomed back in again. The grass was gone, parched earth in its place. A drop of rain fell and slipped between the cracks in the dirt. From it, a seedling grew, its green leaves unfurling like arms stretching toward the sun. It blossomed into a flower. An Artifex knelt down beside it and plucked it from the ground.

"His name is Spark."

Spark. Remi recognized his name—Blee had told her to stay away from him at all costs.

A building appeared where the plant had grown, electric blue glass wrapping silver and purple. More buildings appeared around it. A new city spread out, and tall spires rose. Beacons of light burst from their tops as day turned to night.

A wall began to form around the buildings, rising layer by layer, enclosing the city. Beyond the barrier, the storms raged, howling winds and violent rains. But inside the barrier, a golden-bronze sun shone. And there was peace.

"Welcome to Arcadia," the voice echoed through the theater. "You are safe here. Spark will *always* keep you safe. But—" The voice paused, its tone growing serious. "Remember: living here is a privilege. Spark has created rules for your safety, and for the safety of others. Order can be maintained only by following them."

The screen showed a robot running from a building, a bag in hand, with a crowd of Artifex chasing behind him, waving their arms and yelling.

"Your disobedience will result in immediate removal from Arcadia."

Glowing cuffs appeared around the Artifex's wrists. A shadow spread over him, and a drone came down from the sky. It lowered a hook that slid into the cuffs, and then it lifted off, carrying the Artifex over and beyond the wall.

Remi thought back to the drones she had seen at the warehouse, with bodies dangling underneath. Criminals from Arcadia.

The movie ended with a final shot of the city, the camera moving in a circle around the tall buildings, soaring above the clouds. The word *"SPARK"* was emblazoned across the sky in gold letters.

The screen went dark, and the room with it.

Remi sat quietly, still held fast to her seat, thinking about everything she had just seen.

The screen lit up again. "Many years ago..."

The movie had started over—back at the beginning. Remi frowned, but the other Artifex continued to watch with rapt attention. Happy remained at his post, and presumably Sad still stood guard at the door.

How long do we have to sit here?

But on the second viewing, there was one difference: as the voice droned on, the Artifex mumbled softly to themselves. They were saying the words along with the narrator, their murmur growing. Louder, and louder, and—

Remi felt a change in the room.

There was a hiss of static, and the screen flickered and went blank, as did the Artifex's eyes. She looked around the dark theater, wondering what had happened. Happy stood unmoving at the side of the stage, frozen in place along with everyone else. It was as if time had suddenly stopped.

The screen was filled with digital snow, a sea of blinking pixels. And then, among the snow, appeared an angled face—the face of a woman. Violet rays shone through her polygons, and her eyes and mouth were diamonds of white light. It was a face Remi recognized. She had seen it in one of her visions, in the orchard, on the day she had discovered AJ's brain on the ground. This was the winged creature made of crystal triangles.

"You must listen carefully to me," said the woman. Her voice was warm and commanding, yet there was a weakness to it, a fragility, as if she was making a great effort to speak. "We do not have much time. The infection is in Arcadia now. Spreading like fire from the child."

The child? Remi thought. Then she understood. *AJ.* Arcadia had been virus-free, and then AJ had arrived, bringing the virus with him. He hadn't been here more than an hour or two, and it was already spreading.

And it was all Remi's fault. She had brought him here.

"Where is AJ?" she asked, urgently. "Is he okay?"

The face jerked. Colored lines flashed across the screen, followed by a burst of snow and the sound of static. The voice returned.

"AJ will be doomed like everyone else if you do not hurry. A cure is possible, but only if I'm not infected first. You must get here before the virus does. Otherwise, all hope will be lost."

Remi's words raced to catch up with her mind. "I—I've seen you before. Who are you?"

"My name is Alethea. I am the last of the Elder Minds. What you saw of me was someone else's distant memory—an encounter from long ago. And with that memory, you were given something else…"

"*The primer code,*" Remi said. "It's in my head. But I don't know how to find you." She rattled her arms against the seat. "And right now, I can't even move—I'm stuck here."

Anger flashed across Alethea's face. "I can free you so you no longer have to suffer through this… brainwashing. You must leave this place at once."

The polygons of her face began to stretch and shift, and white light shone through the cracks, which continued to widen. The other Artifex began to stir, and Remi realized why: Alethea's control over the room was fading.

"I cannot hold the signal any longer," Alethea said, her voice strained. Her eyes shifted to the side, as if she was looking at something beyond the screen, beyond Remi's view. Then her mouth curled into a frown. "The virus is here now—in this very building. You must act quickly. Spark is holding me in a prison at the top of the Moonscraper tower." Her face distorted even more, and Remi thought she would come apart at any second. "You will find me there."

"But—"

"You must hurry."

The voice stopped, the room went still, and then came a loud crack, and a spider web of light splintered Alethea's face. She exploded in a radiant burst, sending a blizzard of shards hurtling across the screen.

No sooner had she vanished than the movie came back to life, right where it had left off, as if someone had pushed play. The glow of the Artifex's eyes returned, and the bots resumed their murmuring, oblivious to what had just happened.

But Alethea kept her promise. With a click, Remi felt the pressure on her arms release. She lifted an arm and wiggled her fingers. She was free.

At her movement, the Artifex next to her turned to look. Remi quickly flung her arm back against the armrest, pretending nothing had happened. The robot turned away and looked back at the screen.

Nothing to see here, Remi thought.

She was free of the chair, but she was still surrounded by Artifex, Happy and Sad, and any number of Leaks outside the locked doors. She needed an escape plan.

As she wracked her brain, trying to think of an idea, she thought she heard a scratching noise. She focused, trying to block out the narrator, the music—and heard the noise again. It was coming from behind the screen. She looked at Happy, wondering if he had heard it too, but the bot continued to stare vacantly at the crowd. Then, looking back at the movie, she saw the picture ripple.

Something was pressing against the screen from behind.

The scratching turned to tearing. A hole appeared near the bottom of the screen, and gray fingers poked through, curling around the fabric.

A Leak.

As its cry echoed through the theater, the movie played on, now showing the image of the burning world. Another hand appeared, and the two hands pulled the screen apart, tearing open a long gash that split the screen, and the world with it, right down the middle. Writhing arms pushed through, then a head, howling over the soundtrack.

The Leak fell onto the stage, its fingers scraping the floor.

Remi jumped to her feet, no longer worried about being spotted by the goons. Oddly, the robots in their seats seemed completely unaware of the intruder, but Happy reacted.

He ran toward the exit.

The Leak was too fast. It leapt through the air with a cry, landing on Happy and bringing him to the ground, head pulsing and eyes flashing.

Remi had seen enough. She spun around. The theater doors were wide open, and Sad was missing from his post. She bolted into the aisle.

An alarm began to blare from outside the door. The movie cut off and the room went dark, and Remi saw the red eyes of the Leak. It has abandoned Happy—and was now coming for her.

She sprinted up the aisle, through the door, and into the hallway, slamming the doors shut behind her. The candles flickered, the siren screamed, and in the confusion, she wondered where Sad had run off to. She was afraid of the Leaks, but she didn't feel too secure about the idea of the goon lurking somewhere in the shadows, either.

The hallway to the left would take her back down to the train. She ran to her right.

A bright sliver of daylight appeared ahead, far away. A way out of this horrible place—finally. Remi ran toward it. If she could escape, she would find Alethea. She would make sure of it. She just had to keep going.

"Help!"

Remi stopped. The voice had come from behind a closed door. She walked back to it and put her hand on the knob.

"Help!" She was so close now. Just a little bit farther and she would be free. *Keep going,* she told herself—but she couldn't. Someone needed her help.

Remi cursed under her breath and turned the knob.

CHAPTER 18

THE PRISONER

THE DOOR LED to a wide, deep room with empty white walls and harsh overhead lights. Walls of glowing bars divided the room into cells. Remi had stumbled upon some kind of jail.

"Over here," a voice called.

Remi followed the voice to an Artifex inside one of the cells. The other cells were empty.

"I heard noises outside," the Artifex said, pushing his face forward against the bars. He had a wavy line for a mouth, and only one of his eyes was lit up. "Tell me what's happening."

Remi wasn't sure if she could trust the Artifex. He was behind bars, after all, and perhaps for a very good reason. She turned away.

"Wait! Don't leave! I've done nothing wrong."

Against her better judgment, she stopped.

"Please."

Remi decided that whoever the bot was, he couldn't do her much harm locked up. She turned back to face him, and the bot curled his fingers around the bars, causing them to crackle with energy.

"The Leaks are in the building," she said.

The bot gasped. "Leaks? No way—it can't be. What about the wall? It's kept them out for so long…"

She swallowed hard. "They, um, must have found a way in." She wasn't about to explain that she was responsible for bringing the virus to Arcadia.

"Then you must help me get out of here." The bot's hands rattled against his cage. "You can't just leave me in here. They'll find me."

"But how—"

"There's a key to disable the energy beams. That awful grinning robot has it."

It wasn't hard to guess who he meant: Happy. And Remi had just seen him attacked by a Leak. "That's going to be a problem," she said. "He's been infected."

Then again, Remi thought, after AJ had been infected, it had taken him a few minutes to feel the effects. Perhaps Happy wasn't completely transformed yet? If she could make it back into the theater…

She couldn't believe she was even thinking about this. Happy was dangerous enough *before* he was infected. And he was surrounded by a room full of Artifex who were likely infected by now, too. Plus, who knew how many more Leaks had come through the hole in the screen?

Remi made up her mind. "Don't give up yet," she said to the trapped bot.

"Wish me luck."

XOXOX

The first thing Remi noticed was that the alarms had stopped. In their absence, the nightmarish howls of the Leaks echoed clearly down the hall. She paused in the doorway, gazing down the dark, endless corridor, listening to the sounds. A light flickered from what she thought was the theater entrance. That was no doubt the source of the wails. At least the hallway appeared empty.

Although she dreaded the idea of returning to the theater, and Alethea had insisted she leave, she would never forgive herself for leaving the robot stranded helplessly in the cell.

She stepped out from the door, closing it behind her, and crept quietly down the hall, her senses on overdrive. She trained her eyes on the shadows, keeping a lookout for anything unusual, hoping to spot a Leak before it spotted her. Not far in, she nearly tripped over something on the floor: a speaker with tangled wires pooling beneath it. The Leaks must have ripped it from the ceiling; that explained why the alarm had stopped.

The cries grew louder as she moved toward the theater.

She saw the old wooden doors in front of her.

A long, anguished wail sounded from beyond them.

Her footsteps grew slower.

Almost there.

She moved cautiously forward, leaned around the door—and saw Sad barreling toward her.

She didn't have time to react. The robot slammed into her, knocked her to the floor, and loomed over her with his terrible frown. He started to lean over, to reach for her, when a shriek came from just behind him. Sad stood quickly and raced away down the hall. A Leak burst from the theater and chased after him.

Remi took a second to catch her breath, then entered the theater. The movie was still playing, but barely: it cut on and off, flashing random frames onto the torn screen. The Leaks were gone—she breathed a sigh of relief—but the infected Artifex still sat in their seats, their bodies writhing and their arms and legs twitching frantically. They had clearly been infected by the Leaks, and now the malicious code was working its way through them. Remi expected them to rise up at any moment, animated by the virus that had filled their empty minds with madness. The sight of them made her second-guess her decision to return, but it was too late now.

On the stage, dragging himself toward the gash in the screen, was Happy, apparently trying to escape. To where, she had no idea, but the virus was in him too, and the low, guttural whine he emitted was a warning that his time was almost up.

She climbed onto the stage, sneaking up behind him. She did her best to be quiet, but she couldn't stop her suit from scraping across the floor. When she snatched the key card from his hip, he was in no position to resist; he merely turned his head to look at her, his mask half gray, then resumed his crawl toward the screen.

She had what she had come for. She turned to leave.

And then she heard the sound she had been dreading: the deadly chorus of infected Artifex.

The audience had come to life.

The Artifex-turned-Leaks were howling and moving, their heads jerking erratically. They were rising from their chairs and picking themselves off the floor, wobbling like tops, trying to gain their balance. Without hesitating, Remi jumped from the stage, card in hand, and ran up the aisle and out the doors. She sprinted down the hall to the room where the prisoner waited.

The door to the prisoner's room was ajar. A shiver ran down her spine; she was certain she had closed it firmly when she had left earlier.

She stepped closer and peeked into the crack. There was a Leak inside, moving about wildly, clawing at the bars and hissing in a frenzy. The Artifex cowered in the corner of his cell, putting distance between himself and the crazed machine.

Remi pressed her back against the wall and took a deep breath. She felt her heart hammering in her chest and once again considered running for the exit. It was wide open, waiting for her. She could just walk through it. But as tempting as it was, she knew she had to help the Artifex. She couldn't just leave him here.

Then she remembered the broken speaker. She went back and picked it up, then returned to the prisoner's door.

This had better work.

She screamed as loud as she could, stepped to the side of the door, beside the hinge, and waited.

She heard the Leak's footsteps coming toward the door. As soon as the door opened, she flung the speaker as far as she could down the hall. It landed with a crash in the darkness and skidded across the floor. The Leak sped off after it, howling as it went.

Remi slipped into the room. "I've got the card," she said, proudly.

The bot leaped up and pushed its face against the bars. "The lock panel is over there, on the wall! Hurry!"

Remi waved the card in front of the panel. With a click, the bars vanished.

"Thank you!" the bot said, rushing to the door. He leaned out and peered into the hall. "All clear."

XOXOX

Remi and the Artifex stepped out into a long alley. The crowded buildings towered over them like monolithic guardians. Remi craned her head back, letting her gaze follow the structures to the sky. They seemed to rise forever, and she could see only pale slivers of midday light in the cracks between the tops of the high rises conferring overhead. The light that did make it through faded long before it reached the ground, leaving them in near darkness.

Remi felt overwhelmed, standing in their looming shadows. There had to be thousands more such buildings, just as large, filling the walled island of Arcadia. What hope did she have of finding Alethea in this place?

Walking together down the alley, they came upon three Artifex huddled around a burning drum. Their eyes were vacant, their bodies frozen. They stood like mannequins and appeared to be in some kind of a trance.

"What's wrong with them?" Remi asked.

"NoOps," the Artifex prisoner said. "That's what they're called. Spark's formatting doesn't always work. And when it doesn't…" His boot splashed down in oil. "They end up like this. Come on." He led her around the unmoving machines and crackling flames. "We're better off leaving them alone."

"Formatting?" she asked, looking over her shoulder as the bot pulled her forward.

"You saw that movie, didn't you?" the bot asked.

Remi nodded.

"That's what he calls that movie: *formatting*. But it's more like brainwashing. Ever since we started wising up to Spark's ways and fighting back, he's been replacing us old-timers with new Artifex, a new population to rule over. They get formatted by that movie so they know how to do one thing: follow his orders."

The Artifex stopped and looked at her suspiciously.

"You aren't one of them, are you?"

Her pulse quickened. She shook her head.

"Anyway," the prisoner continued after a pause. "None of that matters anymore now that the Leaks are here—inside the wall."

They continued down the alley, and Remi's sense of dread grew with each step. They heard the cries and screams of the infected robots, but it was impossible to tell where they were coming from. Here, in the cold and the dark, they could be anywhere.

The alley ended at a narrow street. Piles of broken glass lay on the sidewalk across the street, apparently having fallen from the many broken windows above. Fires burned behind some of those windows, and the air was tinged with smoke.

The Leaks had been here.

The prisoner looked around nervously, then started down the street to their right.

"Where are you going?" Remi called.

"Anywhere but here."

She hurried after him. At the moment, he was the closest thing she had to a friend in this unfamiliar place.

They came to a break in the buildings where the sunlight shone through, its warm rays burning away the shadows. The Artifex stopped and studied Remi in the light.

"You're different from the other Artifex," he said matter-of-factly. "You ask too many questions…"

Remi tensed and took a step back. Did he know her secret? What had given her away?

"Relax," the Artifex said. "I don't know how you managed to get into that theater, or why you were there. And I don't really care. You saved my life, and I owe you." The Artifex held out his hand. "The name's Hue."

She paused, wondering if she could trust him. Then again, what did she have to lose?

She shook his hand. "I'm Remi. And I came here looking for the Moonscraper."

"The Moonscraper?" Hue's eyes darkened and he shook his head. "You don't want to go anywhere near that place." His tone sent a shiver down her spine.

"Why not?" she asked, not sure she wanted to know the answer.

"That's where Spark lives. And if you don't already know that—well, maybe you don't know how terrible he is. Trust me, this guy is bad news."

"That's what I've heard," she said. "But I don't have a choice; I have to go there. Do you know where it is?"

He shrugged. "Well, I'm not sure taking you to Spark's home is repaying a debt, but if that's what you want… Yeah, I'll show you where it is. It's the tallest building in Arcadia, so it's hard to miss. Come with me"

The bot led her down the street to a flight of stairs going up. Hue looked around, as if worried they were being watched, then proceeded up the steps. At the top was an empty stone courtyard with a great view of the city.

"Look over there," Hue said, pointing.

Remi gasped. Rising from the city was the tallest building she had ever seen; its top disappeared into the clouds. It was shaped like an obelisk, with simple, straight lines, and the sunlight glistened against its golden sides.

"You're looking at the Moonscraper," Hue said. "But I'm telling you: you should stay as far away from that place as you can. It's the best advice I can give you."

"Thank you—but my mind is made up. It's something I have to do," Remi said.

"Well in that case," he said, sighing, "the least I can do is help you get there. Like I said before, you saved my life."

"I'd appreciate that."

"Let's stick to the side streets," Hue said. "The Leaks are bound to be all over by now. Better we stay out of sight."

He led the way through the city, choosing back streets that were well lit. Remi soon lost all sense of direction, but Hue moved forward with unflinching purpose.

"So, why were you in that cell, anyway?" Remi asked.

Hue glanced back at her. "They were keeping me there while they waited for deportation," he said, keeping his voice low.

"Deportation?"

"Yeah. Disagree with Spark, and that's what happens. They just toss you right out of here. Or fly you, rather—strapped to the bottom of a drone. You see, I used to be somebody around here—back when the city was still alive, before Spark started replacing everyone. But then my friends started disappearing one by one. At first, I made excuses for Spark, thought they had done something to deserve it. But then something happened that changed my mind."

"What?" Remi asked.

"That monster took a very good friend of mine away, dropped her on the other side. Her only crime was studying the virus, looking for answers. But Spark said not to; said it was wasted effort." He looked down at the ground as he walked. "I want to hope she's okay, but I know she's already been infected. I can feel it. Anyway, a few days ago, I decided to go find her. Which meant

I needed to get myself kicked out of Arcadia. Turns out that's a pretty easy thing to do—all it took was muttering a few bad words about Spark in front of the right people, and the next thing I knew, I found myself in that cell, waiting for my turn."

"Is Spark an Artifex like you?" Remi asked.

"No one's ever seen him, so it's impossible to tell for sure. He runs Arcadia from the Moonscraper—stays holed up there, never leaves, lets his henchmen do his dirty work. But whatever he is, I don't think he's an Artifex. He's way too powerful. He knows everything that happens in Arcadia, everyone's secrets. I don't know any robot like that.

"But it doesn't matter anymore. Arcadia will be gone soon. His shiny empire has come to an end. Karma is returning the favor."

They stopped at an intersection. "Well, here we are."

Just down the street was the base of the Moonscraper. A crowd of Leaks was gathered on the broad steps near the entrance. A few of them moved toward the doors, but a popping sound sent them all scurrying back.

"This is exactly what I was afraid of," Hue said. "There's no way in. You've seen it for yourself. You're better off turning around and going the other way. Escape, or find someplace to hide."

"I can't turn around now, Hue. I have to find a way in."

"Why?" he asked. "I hate to say this, but you don't stand a chance at stopping Spark, if that's your plan. Most of us tried a long time ago; he's way too powerful. His algorithms are too advanced. You're better off trying to get out of here while you can. Turn around, run as fast as you can. Maybe you still have a chance."

"No," Remi said. "There's someone there I have to see. Someone who can save your friend—save you all. But she needs my help."

Hue stared at her. "Nothing can save us now."

"You're wrong. There is a cure. And it's inside that building."

"A cure? That's impossible. And even if a cure did exist, there's no way to reprogram us once the virus takes over. It locks the mind up while it destroys it from the inside. We've tried everything."

"Not everything," Remi said. "I have a key."

Hue laughed. "A key? What are you talking about?"

"I have the primer code."

The robot froze. "That's just a rumor."

"It's real," Remi said. "And it's inside my head."

Hue eyed her suspiciously. "You're crazy. Listen, I thank you once more for rescuing me, but... I think I've heard enough." He turned to leave.

"Wait! I promise you, I'm telling the truth," she pleaded. "And I need your help."

Remi lifted her hands to her helmet, her fingers fumbling. Then she found what she was looking for: a latch.

This is the right thing to do, she thought. *I need his help. There's no other way.*

Her fingers gripped the latch and pulled. With a hiss, the mask was released from the helmet and fell to the pavement. Remi stared at Hue with her own eyes.

The Artifex staggered back. "In all my years... It can't be."

"My friend's father, an Artifex like you, gave me the primer code. I have come here to find Alethea—to find a cure."

"Alethea? The Elder Mind lives?"

"Yes. And she's in the Moonscraper. Spark has her trapped. Now do you believe me?"

Hue's eyes glowed brighter than ever. "So that's where Spark has gotten all his power from. Listen, if what you say is true—if you do have a code that can save us—then I'll do my best to help you. Maybe you can put an end to this, once and for all."

"Maybe," Remi said, smiling, "but I'm not going anywhere like this. Can you give me a hand? I'm kind of stuck right now." Removing the mask had turned off the helmet's control of the suit, and Remi was now frozen below her chin. "Can you reattach that mask? I need it to control the suit."

The bot picked up the mask and pressed it into place. The locks engaged, and he stepped back.

"Thank you," Remi said. "Now—any ideas how we can get inside that building?"

He looked around. "I may have one idea."

He picked up a glass bottle that lay in the littered street. Then he opened a panel on his shoulder, plucked out one end of a tube, and placed it into the bottle. A light blue fluid flowed from the tube, filling the container. "Liquid hydrogen," he explained. "I knew my backup energy reserves would come in handy someday." He grabbed a newspaper, rolled it up, and shoved its crumpled end into the bottle. "I'll get the Leaks away from the door, then it's up to you to figure out how to get inside. Think you can handle it?"

Remi nodded. "I'll take it from there."

Hue unscrewed one of his fingers and held it up. A flame erupted. "Thank you, Remi. I'll never forget what you did for me." He waved the fire over the paper until it caught, then slid around the corner so that he was in plain sight of the Leaks. "Hey!" he shouted. "Over here!"

The distant wails grew louder.

"Come and get me!"

Remi stayed out of sight around the corner. Hue sprinted down the street, away from the Moonscraper, flaming bottle in hand, and moments later a frenzied group of Leaks came following after. When they had passed, she stepped forward and watched them run down the street and around a corner. Moments later she heard the explosion and felt the ground shake.

Hue!

She hoped he hadn't been caught in that explosion himself.

But he had done what he had promised: the entrance to the Moonscraper was clear. She thanked him silently and ran to the tower.

She felt a sudden rush of adrenaline as she climbed the broad steps toward the doors, knowing that Alethea waited at the top. She was so close now.

A rifle and camera were mounted just above the gold-framed doors, mirroring her every movement. *Spark's security system.* Remi recalled the pops she had earlier, when the Leaks had moved too close to the entrance. She closed her eyes, waiting for it to fire at her, too, but it didn't.

Instead, she heard the doors open.

CHAPTER 19

SPARK

THE DOORS whooshed shut behind Remi as she stepped into the lobby. Her footsteps echoed across black marble tiles with rich golden veins—a lightning storm frozen in stone. Grand walls of bronze and steel soared around her, and straight ahead was a fountain with a statue resting on a golden perch, a proud Artifex dragging a fallen Neurogeist by its steel tentacles. Water flowed from the Artifex's feet and collected in a pool at the base. High above the fountain was a crystal chandelier that cast diamonds of sparkling light across the room. It was beautiful, but the air was uncomfortably warm and stuffy, as if it hadn't been disturbed in years.

Beyond the fountain, at the far end of the gigantic lobby, was a reception desk. Remi walked toward it.

She was mid-step when she heard a rap on the glass behind her. She spun around and found one of the Leaks standing at the doors with its face and hand pressed against the glass. It twisted its head when it saw her, letting its fingers slide down the glass. But then another pop sounded, and the robot zombie scuttled away.

Feeling deeply unsettled, Remi continued to the reception desk. Behind it, a robot in a leather chair sat with its white plastic arms spread over a honey gold desk. The light was low, and a shadow fell across its upper body, obscuring the bot's face.

"Good morning," the bot said, its motors creaking to life. "And what a pleasant surprise!"

"I need to find Alethea," Remi said. *No point hiding my intentions now,* she thought.

"Alethea?" the robot said. "Why, I've never heard of her." Its voice was coy though, and Remi caught a brief glint in the shadows of its face. One of its dark eyes catching the light, perhaps.

"You're lying. I know she's here."

"That's absurd. Who would put such a ridiculous notion in your head?"

"*She* did."

There was another rap on the doors, loud and sharp. The noise startled Remi, but she quickly regained her composure.

"I need to see her before it's too late. I have something that can save the Artifex."

The bot kicked its legs up on the desk and eased further back in the chair, back into the shadows. "Save the Artifex? How interesting. Do tell…"

The bot was stalling. Remi didn't have time for this. "Where is Spark?" she demanded.

"He's otherwise occupied at the moment. Off on important business. Anything you have to say to him, you can say to me. Now. Just what is that you think can save us?"

More rapping sounded on the doors.

"Ahem—will you hold that thought?" the robot said. "Please excuse me for a second. Seems we have some uninvited guests."

The robot waved a finger over a row of buttons on the desk, back and forth, then let it fall on a large red button. A series of pops sounded outside, and the rapping stopped.

"Now—as you were saying?"

Something was seriously wrong with this bot. There was no

way Remi was going to tell it about the primer code. She'd have to find Alethea on her own.

"I—um, I'm sorry to have bothered you," Remi said, backing away from the desk. "I'll just be leaving now."

But as she began to step away, she stopped cold. Someone was already there, waiting for her, and she recognized its horrible frown at once.

Sad.

"I think you've met my friend," the receptionist said, steepling its fingers. "And he's pretty upset about what happened to his partner back there at the theater. I told him who's responsible..."

Sad stepped closer, menacingly.

"Hold on there just a minute," the receptionist said to Sad. "I have some business with the young lady first." The receptionist cracked its knuckles and spoke to Remi. "We can dispense with formalities. I already know what you have, and why you're here. I know you have the primer code."

The receptionist leaned forward, bringing its head at last into the light. It was missing its mask, leaving only a tangle of wires and disfigured electronics in its place. Its eyes were a sickly green. Now that Remi could see its mangled face, she wanted nothing more than to look away.

"I'll make you a deal," the bot hissed. "Give me the code, and I'll let you walk out of here alive."

Remi's body was trembling inside the suit, but she wasn't about to give up now. "No thanks," she said as confidently as she could.

"Fine," the bot said, retracting its arm slowly. "I knew you'd say no. But I do think it's a rather generous offer, considering you've ruined my life's work by bringing the Leaks here. You alone are responsible for destroying *my* city."

"*Your* city? You're—you're *Spark*?"

"It took you long enough to figure that out," the bot sneered. "You humans are so slow."

"Take me to Alethea," Remi demanded.

"Sorry, can't do that," Spark said, shaking his head.

"Why? Why don't you want to help the Artifex? The Leaks will destroy you too."

Spark laughed. "You want me to stop the virus? Why would I try to stop something *I* started?"

"What?" Remi couldn't believe what she had just heard. "You *started* the virus?"

"Well, maybe I'm stretching the truth a bit..." Spark said, mysteriously. "As much as I'd like to take credit, I guess you could say it was more of an accident. A very *fortunate* accident that emerged from my puppet."

"From your puppet?" Remi asked.

"Her name is Kore—and you already know her. She made short work of your car back in your world. You can thank *her* for the virus."

He leaned his vacant face forward.

"It's actually quite amazing, isn't it? The virus—infecting everything, ripping apart systems from the inside out, altering their programming until primitive emotions are all that remain. Fear. Anger. Aggression. And it couldn't have happened at a better time. My citizens began to fear me, and one by one, they fled my city. I needed a way to regain control. Luckily, the virus gave me exactly that.

"As it spread, I built a wall to protect this city—to keep the wolves from the sheep. Only I could keep them safe. Now the Artifex begged to get *into* Arcadia rather than *out*.

"Poof! Problem solved. Of course, then I learned about something even better—the ultimate form of control. The primer code." He eyed Remi hungrily. "I sent Kore after it, but she failed to do her job. Things didn't work out quite the way I expected, but I do have the code now, don't I? Even if I had to lose my city to get it. Thank you for bringing it to me."

"You're a monster," Remi said.

"Oh, I'm far more than that now. This"—the bot pointed to

himself—"is only the smallest fraction of who I really am, a vestige of what I once was. A helpless Artifex seeking revenge."

"Revenge?"

"The Elder Minds took my wife many years ago. I swore I would destroy them no matter what. But then someone else took care of that for me, and they were all gone. All except one."

"Alethea," Remi said.

"Right again. She was lost at the caves of the Heap, but it didn't take long to find her. I followed the child bot, AJ, and his human friend, Nova, to the caves when they went looking for her. I waited until he'd found her, then I stole her from him, and left him there to die. He never saw it coming."

Remi remembered that AJ had been missing for over three years. She felt sick to her stomach, imagining him trapped by himself for so long.

"From the caves, I fled to this island," Spark continued. "At first, I thought it best to destroy Alethea, but then I came up with an even better idea—a way to harness her power, to use it for my own advantage. By tapping into her mind and stealing her energy, I grew stronger—I created Arcadia—I began to transform…"

The bot reached up with both hands, and to Remi's horror, detached its faceless head with a click, then set it on the desk, wires pooling beneath it.

When it spoke again, its voice came from everywhere at once. "I am everything now. And…" The wall sconces extinguished, one by one, sending a wave of darkness rippling down the lobby. "I am everywhere."

In the back of her mind, Remi registered a clamoring against the door; the rapping had been replaced by a storm of plastic fists.

"I don't care what you are," she said to Spark.

"You *will*!" he screamed. "Get the code from her!" Spark snapped at Sad. "I have the end of the world to attend to."

Then Spark's eyes dimmed, and his presence was gone.

Sad walked toward Remi, raising his arms as he approached. Remi walked backward, keeping her eyes on the goon.

A burst of static came from her helmet's speaker, and then a familiar voice. "I can help you."

Alethea.

"Don't let them know you can hear me," Alethea said. "Move toward the doors—slowly."

Remi heard the pounding on the glass, and hesitated. The Leaks were swarming out there, and getting closer to them was the last thing she wanted to do.

"Trust me," Alethea said.

Sad was closing in on Remi—she had no choice.

She moved toward the door, matching Sad step for step, until she felt her back hit the glass behind her.

"Run when I tell you," Alethea said.

Remi nodded.

"One."

Sad stepped forward, closing in. Remi felt sweat trickle down her forehead.

"Two."

Remi stared up into the void that was Sad's awful, carved frown. Her body was shaking. The bot reached for her.

"Now!"

Remi lunged forward, barely passing under Sad's grip. The robot was caught off guard, stumbled, and smacked into the glass.

The doors opened.

Wails, confusion, and chaos spilled into the room. Remi ran, but glanced back just long enough to see Sad being dragged from the lobby. He clung valiantly to the door frame, but the crowd was too strong. His fingers slipped, and the bot was gone.

"Turn left at the desk," Alethea said.

Remi followed Alethea's directions to an elevator. The doors parted as she approached, and she stepped inside. The doors slid softly shut behind her.

The elevator had dark wooden walls and plush red carpet.

A golden half-moon with black notches sat above the door, its glowing pointer all the way to the left. Buttons completely filled the spaces on both sides of the doors, hundreds of them, from floor to ceiling, all out of order. Two buttons were larger than the others: arrows for up and down.

"Just go up," Alethea said. "I'll take you where you need to go."

Remi raised her finger to press the up button—when Spark's voice interrupted.

"Not so fast," Spark said. "I'm still in a generous mood, so consider this a warning. Alethea is the only reason you're alive right now. But there's only so much she can do, and I promise you this: you'll regret going any further. Step out of the elevator now, and I'll let you live."

The door opened again. From here, Remi could see the headless robot still sitting at the desk.

Not a chance.

She pressed the up button. The door slammed shut, and the elevator began to rumble and lift. The dial above the door wound slowly, tracing an arc from left to right, and the buttons on the sides lit randomly as they moved between the floors.

Suddenly, the elevator jolted to a stop. The lights flickered, then went out. One of the buttons continued to glow in the darkness, telling her where she had stopped.

The thirteenth floor.

Alethea's voice returned. "From now on, I can only protect you inside this elevator. I've used what little energy I had, and I am weak now. Remember: no matter what Spark says or shows you, do not leave the elevator until you reach me."

And the voice was gone.

The doors opened and a blinding light shone in, rippling and electric. Remi recognized it as a door—the same kind of door she had entered this world through. As she peered at it, the elevator walls dissolved, letting the blue light fill her vision. She had to shield her eyes.

The light moved forward, growing brighter still, until a clear membrane formed at its center: a window that pushed the light to the edges of her vision. Her pupils adjusted, and the world behind the door came into focus. The effect was disorienting; she felt like she was somewhere else entirely.

How is this possible?

She was staring at her own driveway, her home in the background, circles of yellow light against the brick. Her father stood off to the side, his head in his hands. Her mother was speaking with someone Remi didn't know. Her brother was there too, pacing back and forth.

Her chin and lips quivered at the sight, and her eyes misted over. "Mom? Dad? James?" Her words came out as whispers, and were carried away by the door's gentle wind.

"This isn't real," Remi said, but she doubted herself.

"Are you sure?" Spark replied. "All you have to do to find out... is step forward."

Remi squinted, trying to see more. A car parked at the end of the driveway flashed blue and white.

And Remi understood. Her mother was talking to a police officer. Remi wanted to race through the door, pull her family close, and tell them all she was okay. Everything would be okay. Her mom and dad would be angry, but they would understand. Maybe even James... And Liv—

Remi's heart stopped. *Where is Liv?*

She almost leapt forward through the cold flame. But she pulled back at the last second, remembering Alethea's warning.

"James?" she yelled. Her voice sounded distorted.

It's no use. There's no way he can hear me. This isn't real.

Then her brother raised his head and looked in her direction. He had dark circles under his eyes, and his ghastly appearance made her shudder. "Remi?" he asked.

"James!" Her voice faded in the wind from the door, but he clearly heard her.

"Is that you?" James raised his hand toward the light, and she saw his fingers touching the membrane. If this was an illusion, it was as real as anything she'd felt: a nightmare that had bled into her waking thoughts.

Remi reached out to him, but he pulled his arm back before she could make contact.

"You have to come back, Remi. Something terrible has happened."

She felt her heart stop, went to cover her ears so she wouldn't hear the news.

"The night you vanished, Liv left the house looking for you. She's gone missing."

"You aren't real!" Remi screamed.

Her brother staggered backward, looking hurt. "Of course I'm real. You need to help us. Come home, Remi!"

"I can't!" she cried, staring down at her feet. How easy it would be to walk forward, run into her parents' arms, and end this nightmare once and for all. But then, that was exactly what Spark wanted.

James's expression changed; he looked angry now. "It's all your fault this happened," he said. "All your fault…"

"My fault?" Remi shook her head. "How could you say something like that?" She knew he was right. But to hear him say it… His words hurt more than anything. "I didn't mean for any of this to happen—you know that."

"Come back now, Remi. Make this right!"

Remi's mom turned away from the officer and stared at her. Her face was pale. Her father turned toward her as well, and together, they joined James by the light. Her parents looked older and more tired than Remi could ever remember.

"Come home," they all said.

Remi lifted her foot, ready to step forward.

"Yeeessssssss…" a voice hissed.

Spark.

The spell was broken. Remi planted her foot firmly back on the floor—inside the elevator.

"No," she said. "I'm not going anywhere. This isn't real."

The air grew cold and still, and a scream sounded all around her. The forms that had once been her family dissolved into dust that scattered. The doors grinded shut, and the elevator continued its ascent.

The golden hand resumed its course across the dial, and Remi wondered how long it would take to reach the top. Then she came to a stop once more.

The doors opened into a dark room with a long row of windows lining the back. It was empty except for a single chair. And sitting in the chair, with glowing ties around his arms, feet, and mouth, gray from the virus... was a robot.

AJ.

His eyes were crimson now, and they stared right at her. Another of Spark's tricks? She wasn't sure, but her heart broke all the same. AJ's expression was strained, his body twitched, but the ties kept him in place.

A face slid out from the side, dark and wretched, made of scraps of plastic and steel fused together in the contours of a skull. Broken shards of metal formed its teeth and round hollowed pits were its cheeks. Cables lashed about from behind it like snakes, and fans exhaled huge gusts of air that kept it afloat.

It glided toward Remi and stopped just before the elevator doors. Its eyes were like mirrors, and she saw reflections of herself staring back at her.

"I'm losing my patience with you, Remi Cobb," the face said, in Spark's voice. "The Leaks are in the building now. We are running out of time!" The face rocked back, and its mouth curled into a snarl full of jagged teeth. "You brought them here! Listen—do you hear them calling? Do you hear their cries at the door?" The face shook, and the room shook with it. Then its anger faded, and it smiled. "I hope you like my present to you. We found him wandering the streets earlier."

The face moved to the side so that Remi would have a clear view of the bot wriggling in the chair. She tried to convince herself that this was illusion. It had to be.

"He's not real," she said. But AJ looked real enough. Far more real than the projection of her family Spark had created earlier.

"Oh, I assure you he's the real deal. Real—and infected." The face moved beside AJ, its eerie eyes glaring down at him. "Now pay attention, because time is running out. Step into the room and gather up your friend here—and you may still have a chance to make it out alive. Keep going up, and I promise you, you'll never find your way back down. All you have to do is step forward. Your choice."

AJ's eyes darted wildly around the room now, and even in the restraints, he jerked so that his chair shook.

He's just an illusion, she told herself again. Still—she was growing less and less convinced of that. She remembered Alethea's warning about staying in the elevator, but if she didn't do something...

The restraints on AJ fell aside, and the bot fell from his chair. He struggled across the floor toward the elevator, and she saw the pain in his red eyes. Even if he was real... it was already too late.

I'm sorry, AJ.

She pushed the button to go up.

The doors began to slide shut. But as they did, for just a moment AJ's red eyes flickered green.

Her friend was still in there.

"Wait!"

Remi shoved her arms through the doors, pulled them apart, and stepped out of the elevator.

"You've made an unfortunate mistake!" The awful face roared, venom dripping with each word. Remi heard a low hum, and her feet stuck to the floor as if pulled by an invisible force.

She was trapped.

Spark's mechanical face pushed closer to her, its mouth curling into a hideous grin. It grew before her, until she stared at the emptiness between its sharp and uneven teeth. "Tell me, Remi Cobb. What do you know about fear?"

"More than you know," Remi replied, balling her fists.

The face laughed, and it was one of the worst sounds she had ever heard. "Let's find out, shall we? I'll have my code now."

Spark's eyes began to glow and pulse, and Remi had the strange sense that this had happened before. She felt her mind growing cloudy, and knew she was starting to lose herself. She felt her eyes close, yet images flashed before her, distant memories pulled to the surface. She struggled to keep them from him, but she was losing the fight.

Then, through the fog, a noise came from... somewhere else. She had heard it before.

An eagle's screech.

The face spun away, toward the sound.

Remi blinked, opened her eyes, and the trance was broken.

In front of her, sliding up behind the wall of windows, was a massive bird, its wings beating with a silent thunder. A shadowy figure stood atop it, midnight black against the fires that burned in the buildings beyond.

The figure leapt through the window, shattering it, and the eagle lifted away.

And then Remi saw its robot arm.

It was the creature. The half-human, half-robot creature that Spark had created. But the scarf was gone. And her face...

She looked just like Nova.

Spark roared. "You should not have come here, Kore! You are under my control—I brought you back to life, and you will do as I say!"

"Not anymore," the creature named Kore yelled. She raised her robot arm and slammed it straight through the mouth of the face, sending up a fountain of sparks. She tore her arm free, then grabbed hold of a spot behind its eyes, and the face howled in agony.

"You should be able to move now," Kore shouted at Remi. She was struggling to hold the face, which was lashing wildly about. "Take your friend and find Alethea. Maybe she can help him. Time is running out." Bolts of electricity twisted around her arm.

"Go!"

Remi ran to AJ and put a hand under his shoulder. And the instant she touched him, a vibration pulsed through her suit. *The virus.* AJ had told her that anything electronic could be infected. Remi herself was immune, but her suit would be ruined.

AJ lifted his face and looked into her eyes, his mouth open in pain, as if he were trying to cry out.

"It's okay, I'm here," she said, lifting her friend and carrying him on her shoulders. She used the strength of the suit to hold him in place.

The building rumbled as Remi trudged toward the elevator. She ignored the crashing behind her and just kept moving. When she was inside the doors, she turned. Kore was now standing over the face, pinning it to the ground with her boot.

"Thank you," Remi said. She pressed the button, and the doors shut.

They were headed up.

CHAPTER 20

ALETHEA

DING.

When the elevator doors slid back, Remi felt a rush of emotions: excitement and relief mixed with adrenaline and lingering fear. After everything she had been through, she had made it to her destination.

The top floor of the Moonscraper.

Stepping into the room, she heard the buzz of electricity and the pops of static discharge. Glass walls sloped together to a steeple far above, and from that steeple, brilliant rays of violet and plum shone down on the hologram of a winged woman.

Remi stood face to face with an Elder Mind.

The woman drifted languidly before her, a phantom of shapes and angles, there and yet not fully there, as if she were a spirit caught between worlds. Her arms were crossed over her chest, and the angled polygons of her face revealed anguish within. Her wings crackled with energy, pulled back and bound by chains that glowed white hot.

Remi laid AJ down on the floor before the spirit.

"Hello, Remi Cobb," the woman said, white light pouring from sad eyes. "I knew you would come."

"Alethea?"

"Yes. It is I."

Remi stared in awe at the magnificent creature. "You are beautiful," she said, reaching out her hand. It passed effortlessly through the specter, breaking the image. She turned her hand around, and the light cast patterns down her arm. When she withdrew her arm, the form became whole once more. "Are you a ghost?" she whispered.

The woman's eyes stared back, searching. "This is only my avatar—a hollow projection. I am neither spirit nor physical being. I exist only as conscious thoughts. Everything I am, everything that is left, is in the Glia box beneath me. It is where I continue to exist, and yet it is also my prison. With your code and my cure, we can stop the Leaks. But if I am to help you, I must be freed."

Remi raised her hand to shield her eyes against the hologram's light. She saw the box underneath Alethea's feet. Glowing chains crisscrossed the black steel, and a bundle of cables emerged from a ring in the center. Patterns and symbols were carved into its surface, but she didn't recognize them.

"I am bound by these chains," Alethea said. "They are taking what little energy I have left, feeding Spark with the essence of my being, helping him grow into the monster he has become. Now, I am only a trace of a power once bright. Please help me remove them."

The elevator doors closed, and Remi heard it begin to descend.

"Hurry," Alethea said. "The Leaks will be here soon."

Remi gripped the links with both arms and pulled with all her might. She could feel the energy of the chains surging through her suit, coming in rushing waves. But her suit's strength was not what it was before; the virus was moving through her.

The chains refused to budge.

"Please!" Alethea cried.

Remi tried again. This time she summoned all the anger

within her; all the hurt, loneliness, and emptiness she had ever felt; the worry, the sadness. She channeled it into her arms, everything she had, fighting back the virus.

And the arms of the suit responded.

Her strength grew.

She screamed, and the chains groaned.

Snap.

She sailed backward through the air, broken chains in hand, and landed on her back. Above her, Alethea's great wings unfurled, filling the room.

Remi gathered herself from the floor. A stillness had settled over the room. But in that silence, she heard the motors engage in the elevator shaft.

The Leaks were on the way up.

"What now?" she asked.

"Bring the infected child to me," Alethea replied calmly.

Remi rose to her feet and gathered AJ in her arms. It was a struggle now to carry him; the virus, and the effort of breaking the chains, had greatly weakened her. She laid him down inside the light, beside the Glia box, and stepped back.

Alethea's light grew brighter and expanded outward until it had consumed his body. He rattled against the floor, then fell still as the light returned to normal.

His eyes no longer glowed.

Alethea's voice returned, but her voice was weaker. "I have downloaded a program into the boy. It will analyze the virus, and when it's finished, part of the antidote will be stored in his mind—just as the primer code is stored inside yours. But I can only access the child's mind, and without the primer code, the antidote is incomplete. The two of you must link your minds together. Only then will the antidote code activate, and the Artifex will be saved."

Link our minds? Remi had no idea how to do that. And even more troubling, AJ wasn't moving. "What about AJ—is he okay?" she asked.

Alethea's words came out slow, labored. "I've put the child to sleep for now. It is better that way—he is still infected."

Her avatar began to flicker and dissolve, particles of dust catching the light and twinkling like bits of gold.

"I must leave now. My power is fading, but I will use what little I have left to give you a way out." She paused. "Thank you, Remi Cobb. For everything you've done."

"Wait—"

The projection blinked out, and Alethea was gone.

Remi looked around desperately.

A way out?

She was trapped at the top of a tower that was about to be overrun by Leaks. She had done exactly what she had come here to do: she had gotten the cure from Alethea. But it was useless until the two parts were combined.

Her job still wasn't done.

Behind her, she heard the elevator coming near.

The Leaks.

There was no time to think. She lifted AJ onto her shoulders. Not only was he heavier than ever, but a stiffness was setting into her suit, and she felt claustrophobic at the thought of being trapped inside an inoperable shell. But she still needed this suit, and she struggled forward under her heavy burden, carrying AJ as far away from the elevator as she could manage.

A boom came from outside, and the shockwave rattled the walls. Remi looked down through the glass, and there, hundreds of feet below, hovering horizontally in midair beside the building, was the door of blue light.

Alethea had promised her a way out—but this?

The elevator dinged, and from behind the doors, over the thumping of her heart, Remi heard the buzzing, grating sound of the Leaks.

She had no choice but to jump.

With AJ slung over her shoulder and one arm curled tightly around his waist, she slammed her fist as hard as she could against the glass. A tiny splinter appeared. She hit the wall again. The crack grew into a shattered web. *Almost!*

She tried to punch the wall a third time—but the suit gave off sparks, and her arm stopped midway into her swing.

Not now!

With all her effort, and with a final cry, she pushed her fist into the pane, and the wall shattered, its shards raining into the depths below, around and through the door of light.

Remi peered down. The wind was howling, fires lit the sky-line, and smoke billowed. A wave of fear rushed over her as she thought about what she had to do next.

The elevator doors opened, and the Leaks spilled into the room.

Now or never.

Remi took one last look, swore under her breath—

—and jumped.

CHAPTER 21

KEEPER OF THE DIVIDE

SHE FELL INTO THE ABYSS feet first, wind whipping past her suit. The door of light lay far beneath her like a blanket of icy fire, burning icy cold. She should have been paralyzed with fear, but she had no time to think, no time to worry.

She plunged into the portal, its edges rippling, its brightness filling her vision. She held on to AJ for dear life. Her strength was gone, her muscles weak, but she didn't dare let go.

She closed her eyes and wished the world away.

When she opened them again, her wish had been granted. The light was no more. But she was still falling, plummeting from an unknown height. Expecting to see ground beneath her, she looked down—and saw only a shimmering darkness.

Water.

The sea rose up to touch her feet, and with a splash, it tore AJ from her arms and swallowed her whole. She felt the force of it rushing around her, knew she was going too deep, streaking through the water like a bullet. The suit sustained her with trapped air, but even if she were capable of swimming with the suit on, it was largely unresponsive. She floundered in the murky depths, bubbles lifting from her body.

And then she heard a sizzle, and to her surprise, she felt the sudden chill of water seeping in around her. The suit was beginning to come apart. Perhaps the water was interfering with the electromagnetic locks that held the suit together, or perhaps it was the virus taking its toll. Whatever it was, she was grateful for the release. She took a deep breath, then scrambled to remove her helmet, her arm fumbling for the clasp that held the pieces together.

There.

The lock released, and the helmet fell away. She swam upward, kicking as hard as she could, the rest of her suit breaking away in her struggle.

Free of its weight, she moved faster.

Above her, streaks of moonlight lanced the water.

She swam toward them with all she had left.

The last of her air was running out—and now the light was fading.

Almost there…

With a final, desperate kick, Remi broke the surface and gasped for air.

Her lungs burned as she looked around. AJ was gone, lost somewhere in the froth and churn of the heaving water. The sea lifted to a high crest, and before she fell, she saw the white line of a beach not too far away, steep cliffs behind it. She swam toward it, letting the current and the waves do most of the work, until she felt the sand beneath her feet.

Exhausted, she crawled out of the sea and collapsed.

When she had sufficiently caught her breath, she sat up and gazed over the moon-speckled water beneath the midnight sky. A warm breeze washed over her.

Where are you, AJ? And where am I?

She had passed through the blue door of light, which meant

she was probably in yet another reality. At least she liked it here. This place was calm and peaceful. She could relax, let her problems go.

Stay forever.

This place was having a strange effect on her. She felt the unease and the worry slipping away. Her mind began to wander, her memories fading.

And then a brief glimmer of light appeared down the shoreline. Somewhere inside her, Remi felt a vague notion of responsibility—something she needed to do. She got to her feet in a daze, dusted the sand from her pajamas, and walked toward the light. It felt as though she were stepping through a dream.

She had lost track of time and distance when she reached a pier stretching out over the ocean. A tall, haunted form, cloaked and hooded, waited beside a wooden raft that bobbed in the sea. She walked down the pier toward it, the rotted boards groaning beneath her with each step.

"Where am I?" she asked.

The figure turned its head toward her, and she heard the faint sound of grinding motors. It lifted its arm, and with skeletal fingers, it pulled back its hood to reveal an iron skull, rusted from the salty air. The skull gazed upon her with round black eyes, deep wells of oil that reflected her face. It was chilling, but she was not afraid of it. She was not afraid of anything now.

"You have entered the Void," the machine said. Its voice was deep and gruff, ominous. "The edge of the universe. It is a world of nothing, a bridge to the final reality. I can tell you are weary—but you must make a choice. This place is not meant to be inhabited. Stay too long, and your mind will be lost to the sea."

She was tired… "A choice?" Remi asked, dreamily.

A fire burned within the machine's eyes, and the tip of his staff grew bright. "Yes. Because your route here was most unusual, you have a choice—it is up to you where you go." His words were slow and deliberate. "You may continue on to the usual destination…" He waved his staff toward the silver cliffs. A warm light glowed above them. Without knowing why, Remi found herself longing for whatever waited behind them.

"Or—" he said, bringing his cloak and staff around, so that it pointed out to sea, "—it is possible to take you back, though it will not be easy. You must decide…"

Remi felt more confused than before. "You can take me back? Who are you?"

"I am Hex, keeper of the divide."

Remi gazed over the sea, then looked down at the raft. Images of her family swirled in her head like lost spirits. She missed them. She knew she still had something more to do.

"I choose to go back," she said.

"Very well." Hex pulled his hood forward and spun around to step onto the raft, his cloak swinging after him. "Follow me," he directed.

Remi climbed onto the craft. Flames swelled within crooked oil lanterns that flanked its sides.

"Please, sit," Hex said, facing the sea.

Remi did.

Hex raised his staff into the air. A ring of steel fins grew from its top and began to spin, vanishing in a blur of motion. He lowered the spinning end of his staff into the ocean, and the water began to froth white. The raft sped forward, into the fog that was settling over the water.

Remi felt like they had traveled only a short distance when the raft began to slow.

"You didn't come here alone?" Hex asked, looking over the side of the raft.

Remi followed his gaze. The body of a robot child floated beside them, pale in the moonlight. He looked familiar; she knew him. But she couldn't remember…

Hex lifted the child from the water with ease and laid him gently on the raft. His eyes were still vacant, his body gray and unmoving.

"Someone you lost?" Hex asked quietly.

The question echoed through Remi's mind, and as it did, she remembered who the robot was.

His name was AJ. He was her friend.

"AJ..."

He needed her help. There was something she needed to do, someplace she needed to go...

"We have to go back to Arcadia," Remi said suddenly.

Hex said nothing, only lowered his staff back into the water, and the raft moved forward once more.

They continued for some time, across gentle waters at first, then across the stiff peaks of waves that sent them thrashing about. Remi held tight to the raft. Her memories were returning, and with them, she felt a sense of urgency. She needed to get back.

At last, another shore appeared in the distance, and the iron ferryman slowed. He raised his staff from the water, and the lanterns went dark. "The way home..." He cast his staff forward, and the sky ripped apart. A blue door climbed from the water just ahead of them, and the ferryman's tall body was silhouetted in its light. His cloak billowed behind him as they drew closer...

And then they were through the door, back in the Artifex world.

Though they were still on the raft, still at sea, it was no longer night; the sun was only just setting. In the distance, the wall of Arcadia rose from the sea, a beach spreading below it and a great swirl of smoke above.

The ferryman propelled the raft forward silently until sand scraped underneath it. He lifted AJ and carried him onto the beach, and Remi followed him, feeling more tired than ever.

As Remi slumped down next to AJ, Hex pushed the raft back into the water and climbed aboard. "You are safe here," he said, then departed without another word. He disappeared into a blue light that opened on the horizon.

Remi felt her mind fading. She fought it back as best she could, but sleep was coming.

As her eyes closed, a sudden wind blew against her face and

engines roared overhead. At first, she didn't understand what was happening. Above her, a black triangle was set against a red sky. And then she realized what it was:

A drone, descending toward her.

Her vision clouded at the edges, darkness swelling, and her consciousness slipped away.

XXX

Remi's eyes were still closed when she heard footsteps approaching. They stopped next to her, and a second later she felt a hand against her forehead.

"How is she?" a woman asked. Her voice was familiar.

"She could use some more rest, but I think she's going to make it," said another woman, whose voice sounded nearly identical. "I don't know how they ended up here, but we were lucky to find AJ's signal when we did."

The footsteps moved away, and in their place was a faint hum. Remi rested on a pile of blankets, but underneath it, the floor was rumbling.

She opened her eyes. A metal ceiling hung low above her, with two rows of rivets and a strip of dim lights down the middle. Curved walls bowed out to either side. She was reminded of the cargo bay she and AJ had stowed away in when they had flown into Arcadia.

Then she remembered the drone that had come from the sky. She must be flying inside it.

She rolled over and saw that she was not alone. AJ and Achilles were both just a few feet away. AJ's body lay still on the floor, his eyes still dark.

And Achilles… The dog was in rough shape. His ribs were gnarled, and his body was shaking.

Remi sat up, massaged her head, and scooted over to him. "Achilles?"

When she reached for him, his head snapped up, his eyes flashed red, and he growled.

"It's best to stay away from him for now." It was the voice of the woman from before.

"He was infected at the warehouse," said the second woman with a deep sadness.

Remi looked up. Two women stood before her in the dim light. She didn't trust her eyes. It couldn't be.

Both of them were Nova.

"How—" she asked, her jaw hanging open.

One of the women stepped forward. She wore dark gray pants and a crimson jacket, torn and ripped. A robot arm hung from her side.

"You—" Remi said, shuffling away from her on the floor. "I don't understand." This was Kore: the creature who had destroyed her car, the creature who had attacked them at the warehouse. And the creature who had saved her from Spark.

"It's okay—I promise I won't hurt you," the woman said. "My name is Kore." She nodded at the woman next to her. "I'm Nova's sister."

"Sister?" Remi said. "I don't understand."

"It's true," Nova said. "Although I had no idea until a few days ago."

"Orion, our father," Kore explained, "made two attempts to bring humans back from extinction, both times using the same DNA. His first attempt didn't work—something went wrong. His experiment failed, and he buried my body... as a way to honor me."

"The person Blee saw buried in the coffin..." Remi said, staring at Kore. "It was *you*. Spark brought you back to life, didn't he?"

Kore nodded. "Spark learned of my existence when he broke into Alethea's mind to steal her power. He dug me up and added hardware where my organic systems had failed. He turned me into this half-machine—this monster. And then something unexpected happened: the biological part of me fought against the mechanical, flesh and blood attacking circuits and code. The virus was born from this struggle. It began to spread, and..."

Her voice broke, and Nova put her arm on her shoulder.

"It's okay," Nova said. "It wasn't your fault. And it will all be over with soon. We can fix it."

"There's still one thing I don't understand," Remi said, looking at Kore. "You've been chasing us. You blew up my car, tried to kill me—"

"I'm sorry about that. I didn't mean to do those things. Spark installed a chip inside my head—a chip that allowed him to take over my mind whenever he wanted."

"A mind control device?"

"Yes. He was obsessed with finding the primer code, and he ordered me to find it. I don't expect you to believe me, but it was Spark who was after you—not me." Kore took a deep breath. "Now Spark is no longer in control, and thanks to Nova, for the first time in my life, I'm free."

"What about the mind control chip?" Remi asked.

"It was destroyed by Nova's EMP, back at the bunker," Kore said. "But the blast also damaged the machine half of my body—I almost died. The circuits that gave me life were failing. Fortunately, Nova found me wandering around in a daze. She carried me down into the bunker and saved my life."

"That's why you weren't at the Silver River," Remi said to Nova. "We thought something terrible had happened to you."

"I'm sorry I couldn't join you," Nova said. "It took hours to stabilize her, and by that time, you, AJ, and Achilles were long gone. Kore and I split up and went looking for you. She found you at the warehouse—the Leaks were there, and you were already on the drone, headed to Arcadia."

"I got there too late," Kore said sadly, her gaze shifting to Achilles.

"No—it's not too late," Remi said. "I found her—I found Alethea. She downloaded the antidote code into AJ. And the primer code—it's been in my head the entire time. We can save them now."

Nova stepped forward and offered her hand. "You've been

amazing, Remi, and I know you've been through so much. Kore told me about what happened with Spark."

Remi took Nova's hand, and Nova pulled her to her feet. "What happened to Spark?" Remi asked.

"His entire city was destroyed by Leaks," Nova said. "And now that you freed her, I suspect Alethea will spend an eternity paying him back for what he did. But I have to ask: how did you end up with the primer code in the first place?"

"AJ's father gave me his memories," Remi said, "although I have no idea how. I can't remember what happened. His memories must have messed up my own."

"Well, I'm glad he did," Nova said. "Now we just need to figure out how to get the primer code from your mind, and combine it with the antidote algorithm in AJ's brain. Any ideas how we go about doing that?"

Remi remembered what Alethea had said back at the tower. "Actually, yes. Alethea told me her code would activate if I linked my mind to AJ's. Does that mean anything to you?"

A look of recognition spread across Nova's face. "Maybe," she said.

Nova turned and walked through the door behind her, and Remi now saw it led to the cockpit. Nova made a few adjustments to the controls, then returned. "There's an old satellite transmission tower in an Artifex city not too far from here. The Leaks have damaged it, but I think it still has enough power to send out the cure. We just need to pick up something from the bunker first."

"What?" Remi asked.

"It's a long story, but there's an old machine…" Nova's face darkened. "The Elder Minds used it download minds into Neurogeists. They tried to use it on Achilles, to turn him into one of their monsters, but I stopped them. I used the same machine to enter his mind—to save him." She paused. "I think we can use it to link your mind with AJ's."

Remi grimaced. The idea terrified her.

Nova must have seen Remi's concern in her face. "I know it sounds scary," she said, "but it's our only chance."

XOXOX

The craft glided above a rundown city, sweeping over crumbling buildings and broken terrain. Up ahead, a soaring mast jutted from an asphalt clearing, like a giant needle rising into the twilight sky. *The broadcast tower.* Parts of its metal lattice had been ripped away—the work of the Leaks, no doubt—and it leaned slightly to one side, threatening to fall over, but it hadn't fallen yet.

The craft came to a rest just shy of its base.

Kore slid the door back, and she, Nova, and Remi carried AJ outside and set him down on the pavement. The sun was almost gone, and Remi could hear the cries of Leaks coming from the wreckage of nearby buildings. The sooner they got this over with, the better.

Nova went back into the craft and brought out the device they had retrieved from the bunker, along with a few cables. The device looked like nothing more than a dusty black box with ancient-looking engravings on its top.

Nova set it on the ground in front of AJ and pushed a button. Lights on the box came to life. Nova then attached three cables to the box. One she used to connect the box to the tower, and the second she used to connect the box to AJ.

She took the end of the third cable and handed it to Remi.

Remi eyed it skeptically. It looked like a vacuum cleaner nozzle, except it had glowing rectangular lines that looked like a circuit board. "This thing is safe, right?" she asked, sitting down across from AJ with the device between them.

Nova sighed. "I hope so, but the truth is, I'm not really sure."

Remi frowned. She thought of Achilles, of all the Artifex that needed her help. Then she looked at AJ's unmoving body. It didn't matter whether it was safe. She had already decided.

"Just tell me what I have to do."

"Lie down and hold the cable to your forehead to make the connection. Let me know when you're ready." Her finger rested on a button on the side of the box.

Remi lay on her side on the asphalt. She held the cable in front of her, and it shook in her trembling hands. Then, summoning her courage, she brought it to her forehead. "Ready."

She felt a buzzing in her mind. The last thing she saw before the world left her was AJ lying peacefully beside her.

CHAPTER 22

INNER VOICES

ALL THE LIGHT was gone, blinked out by the suffocating darkness that appeared when she attached the cable to her forehead. Remi tried to look around, but her physical body was no more. She was just a presence now, alone in her mind. Her first reaction was to panic, but she forced herself to relax, to let herself float through the abyss of her consciousness, adrift on currents of thought and tides of memory.

Her mind cleared, and she remembered her purpose.

She thought of Alethea, and no sooner had she remembered her than a crystalline figure appeared, bringing light to the darkness. Her great wings beat silently in the void, and she stared at Remi with hollow white eyes.

"Alethea?" Remi asked.

"No…" the figure replied. "I am only a remnant of her—just a drop of code she placed in the child."

"You are the antidote program," Remi guessed.

The creature nodded. "I am an algorithm, yes, and my analysis is complete: the antidote is almost ready. But you must remember the primer code for the cure to be complete."

"I don't know how," Remi said. "My head is full of memories that aren't mine. The primer code has to be inside one of them, but I have no idea how to find it."

The figure considered this. "I will help you find it, but you must understand, your mind is not like ours. You will experience someone else's memories as though they are happening to you. You will feel like you *are* that person. Your mind may become confused, even lost… It is possible you will not be able to return to yourself. Are you willing to accept this risk?"

"I don't have a choice," Remi said. "We have to save the Artifex."

"You always have a choice."

"Then I choose to go."

"Very well."

)()()(

She felt a thread tugging gently at her consciousness, and then her memories came floating along the cord. She could see them, passing beneath her like frames of a movie. She saw herself as a child, no more than three years old. Her parents were younger, and James was there too, just a boy. The feeling was strange, and she resisted. The pictures began to slow.

"You must let go, Remi," Alethea's algorithm said. "We're not there yet."

Remi did her best to relax. She felt her mind slipping again, and the memories sped up.

The years went by. She saw memories of herself and her brother—and then her sister appeared, as a baby. She saw herself in the hospital, her parents by her side. The memories were rushing past, faster and faster.

Slow down, she thought.

And they did.

She scanned them, one by one, until she came upon a moment in time she had never seen before. She knew at once this memory did not belong to her.

There, she thought. The image froze on her command.

"This is where they begin?" Alethea's algorithm asked.

"Yes."

Remi felt as though she were falling toward the memory. Her mind slipped away from her, and the last drop of her consciousness was extinguished.

XOXOX

When Remi came to, she knew she was seeing the world through someone else's eyes. And she also knew there was someone else within her, seeing what she saw: AJ. He didn't speak, and he didn't have to. Their minds were connected, their thoughts shared.

This memory belonged neither to her nor to AJ, but to AJ's father, Sudo. And though on some level, Remi knew it was not real, it felt as vivid and clear as life itself.

Sudo stood at a window, gazing out at a world on fire. He was thinking about his city. He knew it would be the next to fall to the Leaks, and then Arcadia would be the only city left. The world was ending… and he didn't care. He knew he should, but ever since AJ had gone missing, nothing else mattered. The world had lost its color.

A knock sounded at the door.

"Come in," he said.

An Artifex rushed into his office carrying a dark orb of metal and glass. "We found this outside. It fell from the sky." He placed it on Sudo's desk.

"From the sky? What is it?" Sudo asked.

"One of the Neurogeist eyes," the Artifex replied. "We inspected it, and there's a message inside. Listen." The bot placed his hand on the sphere, and the glass glowed red.

Within her own mind, Remi remembered the eye Nova had shown her. The broken message she had recovered.

The speaker hissed, and then—

"There is hope, Father. Alethea is alive. I know Spark has her. If we can find her, she may be able to save us all. I was trapped, but managed to escape. You must follow the coordinates and bring the primer code with you. I'll be there."

With a final crackle, the message was over.

Sudo lifted his head. "I knew he was still alive!"

"And there's more. We found coordinates inside the eye's circuits."

"Then I'm leaving at once."

)O(O(

Sudo moved through the trees, stepping across damp ground where moss grew like in tufts of wild carpet. It was a moonless night, and the soft glow of his eyes provided the only light.

He stepped from the trees beside a rising cliff face. A shallow stream ran along its base, and he stepped through it, right up to the rock wall. He knew this was spot without needing to check his coordinates. AJ would be here.

A shrub grew beside the wall, and he pushed it aside. Beyond it was the tiny entrance of a cave. He knew why AJ had chosen this place. They had hidden here once, from the Elder Minds, shortly after he had built AJ.

Now he crouched down and stepped inside.

"Father?"

"AJ!" He ran to his son and scooped him up in his arms. "Where on earth have you been?"

"Stuck in a mineshaft… at the tunnels of the Heap." AJ's voice cracked, and he broke into tearless sobs.

"The Heap?"

"It was Spark. He did this to me." The boy looked around the cave as if he expected to find someone lurking in the shadows.

Sudo set his son down, then knelt in front of him and placed his hand on his shoulder. "It's okay, AJ. I'm here now—tell me what happened."

AJ sniffed. "Nova and I, we were at the Heap. We were there to find Alethea. I was off on my own, searching, when I found her, Father. I found her. And then Spark—he snuck up behind me, used some kind of an electrical shock to knock me out. I woke up in a mineshaft, covered by rocks. Spark had buried me there and left me to die."

Remi could feel the anger swelling within Sudo's mind.

"I dug myself out. I didn't think it would be possible, but I did it, every day a little more, bit by bit. It took me three years, but I escaped."

Sudo squeezed his son tight.

That monster. He would find Spark, exact his revenge.

AJ gazed up at his father. "What about the primer code? Did you bring it?"

Sudo's face hardened. He had never mentioned it to his son; only a few people knew of its existence. "Who told you about that, AJ?"

"Nova told me. I found her on my way back."

"Nova? She doesn't know about the code. Only a few Artifex know of its existence."

"No, Father, it was her. She's the one who gave me the Neurogeist eye to send to you. She's kept watch over me—helping me stay hidden from Spark."

Something is wrong, Sudo thought.

"You said you found Nova. Where is she?" he asked urgently.

A voice spoke from the cave's entrance. "I'm right here."

The bush at the entrance to the cave was pushed aside, revealing a figure bathed in a crimson light. It wore a long tattered old coat, a scarf, and leather gloves.

"Nova?" Sudo said.

"Did you bring the code?" she asked.

It had been years since he had seen her. She looked different. And her voice sounded off. Deeper.

The crimson light grew brighter, spilling into the cave. A whistling sounded outside the cave as well.

"I don't have the code," Sudo said.

"Liar!" Nova screamed. "AJ promised me you'd bring it."

She stormed into the cave, grabbed the child, and lifted him from the ground. AJ squirmed, pulled at her arm, trying to get free—and the arm of her coat tore off, revealing a robot arm underneath.

AJ stared at Nova in horror. "Who are you?"

"I am Kore," the creature said.

Remi, watching the memory through Sudo's eyes, knew that Kore was under Spark's control. The mind control chip. But knowing that didn't make it any easier to witness what happened next.

Kore tore a piece of armor from AJ's arm and pressed her robot fingers into his circuits. A shower of sparks filled the room, and AJ howled in pain. She released the bot and tossed him aside; he landed in a crumpled heap, motionless.

"What have you done?" Sudo pushed past Kore and dropped to the ground next to his son.

"I've infected him," Kore said, smiling down on them. "Now you have no other choice. Either give me the code or watch your son descend into madness." She let loose a deep laugh, and Remi heard an awful voice behind it—the voice of Spark.

A flood of thoughts rushed through Sudo's mind. Never had Remi experienced so much anger, and she thought her mind might burst.

He didn't have the primer code—that much was true. He didn't have it, because he had hidden it in AJ's mind when he built him—hidden it where no one would find it. But now he would lose his son, the code, everything—unless…

Sudo twisted the dome on AJ's head until it clicked free. He pulled it from his son's body, stood, and charged straight at Kore, cradling the dome under his arm. She screamed in surprise, and he knocked her backward into the wall of the cave and darted out into the night.

He dashed across the water, ran under the red-streaked sky, raced into the trees. The Neurogeist eyes filled the skies, and their whistling told Sudo they were giving chase.

But he wouldn't fail his son. He ran as fast as he could, faster than his body would let him. The trees swept by in a blur, deeper into the forest. He didn't stop until he could no longer hear the whistling; for a moment, at least, he had managed to outrun them.

But time was of the essence; he had to work fast. He had no doubt that Kore had infected his son with the virus. Which meant AJ had only one chance: Sudo had to burn it from his mind. The damage would cause his son to lose most of his memories—and likely the primer code—but there was no avoiding it if he was to stop the infection.

The dome shook in his trembling hands.

First, the primer code. He unscrewed his fingertip, and a green light shone from its end. He moved it across the dome—across AJ's brain—copying the primer code into his mind as he went.

Then he opened a second finger. Its end glowed white hot. He hated what he was about to do.

"I'm sorry, AJ. In order to live, you must forget."

He touched his finger to his son's brain and held it there until it the dome turned red and emitted a thin wisp of smoke. Then he moved his finger across AJ's brain, racing against the disease, destroying it—and destroying AJ's memories. It couldn't be avoided.

Sudo had just finished his work when the whistling returned. He spun around; one of the eyes was glowing ominously between the trees. He was too tired to outrun it again; and besides, he needed to get AJ's brain to a safe place.

He remembered a door he opened a long time ago, to a place to which he'd sworn to never return. His artificial neurons fired, retrieving the formula for the door at near the speed of light.

He activated it, and with a loud crack, the blue door split the air.

Cradling the dome under his arm, Sudo leapt toward the door— but he wasn't fast enough. The eye sped toward him and exploded into his abdomen. Sudo reeled backward through the portal, smoke trailing behind him.

Through Sudo's eyes, Remi saw the blue door rising in the night sky and the steam hissing as he splashed down in the pond behind her home. She felt the pain he felt, saw his hands reaching out, clutching the dome as he sank into the pond. With his energy drained, he was forced to let go. He sank down until the algae curled and swayed around him.

And then there was only darkness.

> Backup systems engaged.

The water turned green when his eyes lit. A speck of light floated on the surface above. He remembered his son.

AJ.

With the little energy he had left, Sudo lifted himself up and pushed off with his legs. He reached up, grabbed the dome, and pulled it under.

Even his reserves were low; he had little time left. If his circuits went cold, if he died, the primer code would die with him, and all hope of saving the Artifex would be lost. He needed to figure out something fast before his systems failed him completely. With the dome tucked under one arm, he kicked and drifted to the edge of the pond. At the shore, he tried to walk, but his legs gave way, and he collapsed at the base of a tree, still clutching what was left of his son.

His energy was virtually depleted, his body too damaged for repair.

It was over.

And then...

Something moved.

A shadow stood on a hill. A human. A girl.

There was hope.

Remi knew that she was watching herself—that *she* was the girl on the hill. The night she found AJ's head floating in the pond, she had seen something moving under the trees, had gone to see what it was, and had forgotten. Now she was back where it all began.

Finally—

—She remembered what she had lost.

Sudo rose to his feet, took a step forward among the trees.

The girl must have seen him. She was coming down the hill now, moving his way.

His neural nets raced, and an idea burst into existence. Sudo knew the human mind could store data just like a computer.

He could write his memories into her mind, sending images through her eyes.

The primer code would be safe there. Away from the dreaded creature that had done this to him and his son. He didn't know if it would work, or what would happen to her, but he knew he had to try.

He limped forward, under the trees, toward the girl, until he could go no further.

This would be his final act.

The girl stopped before him, hypnotized by his eyes, her brain ready to receive the data.

Their stares locked.

Sudo prepared the transmission…

And the data began to flow. Changing patterns afloat on an emerald sea, symbols that flashed across his eyes and into hers, each one containing precious data. Still more images appeared, flashing by, frame by frame, with striking clarity, memories imprinted from one mind to another.

…01000010101010000101010101010000101010010000111 0
01000011010000101001000000011101100001100001
001011100011000000011010101011000001

The primer code.

Remi watched the girl—Sudo's memory of her—absorb the code, and as she did, she saw the numbers herself, felt the data moving through her mind. The dream world began to shake. The girl's face began to change. Her eyes and mouth began to glow with energy, and she tilted her head back. Beams of white light shot from her eyes into the sky. The light grew around her until the girl vanished into it, and only the beam remained: a great torch shining from the ground.

She heard Alethea's voice calling out above the confusion.

"You have done it, Remi," she said. "The primer code has been received. Now we must upload the antidote for the cure to be complete."

Dark clouds rolled in, darker even than the night. Lightning flashed, and thunder shook the trees. Remi felt AJ's presence much stronger than before, and then he was there—not in the way she was there, inside Sudo's memory, but actually *there*, standing on top of the hill, an unmoving silhouette. His head glowed even brighter than the lightning that flashed around him, and then a beam of data shot forth from his head toward the sky, matching the beam from the girl, burning away the clouds above him.

Remi felt a thousand voices, a thousand cries at once. The noise grew into a dreadful chorus, the trees began to split, the ground shook. The twin beams grew wider, brighter, until they filled her vision.

Then the lightning stopped; the voices stopped. All was quiet now, and once again, her world went dark.

XOXOX

Remi felt something pushing against her arm—her real arm—and opened her eyes. Achilles was nuzzling her. She put hand on his back and sat up, unhooking the cable from her head. She was back on the asphalt by the power plant, with Nova and Kore looking down at her. AJ was there, too, still asleep.

The cries of the Leaks were gone. She looked toward the buildings surrounding them. A few healthy green eyes peered out, then more.

The Artifex were cured. Their plan had worked.

"What happens now?" Remi asked.

"We rebuild," Nova said. "There hasn't been peace here in a long time, but now, thanks to you, our world has a chance."

"I had some help," Remi said, turning to AJ.

The bot was beginning to stir. The gray was gone from his body, and his eyes were the color of emeralds. He sat up and pulled the cable from his head.

"How do you feel?" Remi asked.

"Kind of weird, but I think I'm okay."

"I'm sorry about your father," Remi said. "He loved you very much."

"I think he would be proud of me," AJ replied. "Of us—of what we did." He rose to his feet and stared into the distance. "I know he didn't survive, but his memories just ended... I don't know what happened to him."

Remi pondered his thought. After that night, she had never seen him again. "Maybe it's better that way," she said. "To remember him as a hero who saved your life."

AJ nodded.

"It's time to get you home, Remi," Nova said. She gestured toward the drone.

Remi nodded and hugged AJ. "I'll miss you," she said.

"Me too," AJ replied. "But you never know..."

"You never know," Remi agreed. She pulled back and looked at him with misty eyes. "Do me a favor though?"

"What's that?"

"Try and stay out of trouble. I don't need your brain showing up in my pond again."

AJ laughed. "Sorry—I can't promise anything."

She had turned to leave when AJ grabbed her hand.

"Remi?"

"Yes?"

"I meant what I said on the drone. You are the best friend I ever had."

EPILOGUE

THE PARTY WAS OVER. Remi, Liv, and James busied themselves on the deck, cramming plastic dishes into an overstuffed trash bag and sweeping crumbs over the railing. They had been celebrating the end of summer and the start of school. For most kids, that would be an unusual thing to celebrate, but not these kids, not this year. For the Cobbs, it meant Remi had gotten a clean bill of health, and the doctors had cleared her to go back to school—back to her friends.

More than half a year had passed since Remi had found the strange dome floating on the pond. When she had returned home after her travel to another world, she had found the police swarming her house and her family distraught. And rightfully so. She had been missing for more than a day. The wreckage of the car had been found, and the police suspected she'd taken the car in an attempt to run away from home.

Remi tried being honest with her parents about what had happened; but her story, unsurprisingly, was met with skepticism. And then James came forward and told his parents he had seen the door burning in the back yard, had seen Remi stepping from it the night she returned home. Remi was sure her parents didn't believe either of them, but ever since that night, James had treated her with a kindness she didn't know he was capable of. They still had their fights—of course—but he was different.

When they were done with their cleanup, and Liv had gone inside to get ready for bed, James turned to his sister. "Feel up for a walk?" he asked.

Remi nodded, wondering what was up, and they headed down the stairs and onto the lawn.

"I wanted to say something…" he said, sounding unsure.

"What?" Remi asked.

James fidgeted with his glasses. "I—I'm sorry."

Remi stared at him in shock. "Sorry for what?"

"Sorry for not believing you. The night you asked for my help."

"I *told* you I saw something."

"Don't push it!" he snapped. "And don't ever tell anyone I said sorry, either."

Remi smiled.

"You never did tell me the whole story," James said.

"You never asked," Remi replied. "I know you already think I'm insane."

"True, but—will you tell me anyway?"

They walked down to the pond and sat under the old willow that grew at the edge of the water. There, Remi told her brother the story of AJ, Nova, Achilles, Sudo, and the Artifex.

When she was finished, she found her brother staring at her in disbelief.

"What?" she said. "I knew I should have kept my mouth shut."

"You *really are* insane," he said.

She frowned, and he laughed. "I'm just kidding. You couldn't make up a story like that even if you tried." He paused and scuffed the ground with the tip of his shoe. "So… Do you think you'll ever see them again?"

"I don't know," Remi said, gazing into the night sky. She knew that AJ was somewhere out there, under a different set of stars, maybe wondering the same thing.

She missed her friend.

James yawned deeply, stood, and stretched his arms. "Come on, let's go. It's late, and I'm getting tired." He started heading up to the house.

It was very late, actually. Remi got up, and was about to follow him, when she saw a flash in the water: a green light, far down, deep in the murk. She stopped cold.

"What's the holdup?" James called. "Planning to stay out here all night?"

Remi gazed into the water. "I'll be up in a bit," she said. "I just remembered something I thought I'd forgotten."

A WORD FROM THE AUTHOR

Thank you so much for reading *The Quantum Ghost*. It means a lot that you would give this book a chance, and I hope you enjoyed it. I intended for Remi's adventure to work as a standalone, but if you'd like to read more about Nova, Achilles, and AJ, have a look at *The Quantum Door*, the first book in the series. Already read it? Rest assured that Brady and Felix's story will continue.

I am deeply indebted to the individuals that have lifted *The Quantum Ghost* with their talents. David Gatewood, thanks for making my words shine (I don't make it easy!), and for pushing me when I needed it. Thanks to Ben Adams for another stunning cover—and for some of the moodiest, most stunning illustrations of all time. Proofreading and formatting wizardry are courtesy of Therin Knite. Thank you!

My family provides me with an endless source of encouragement. To my parents, thanks for reading the early stuff that no one else dares touch. Thank you, Lisa, my love and best friend, for helping me chase a dream. And thanks to my three children for keeping me on my toes. Your curiosity, wonder, and laughter fill me with purpose and inspiration. I hope to make you all proud.

Please visit my website at:
jonathanballagh.com

You'll find links to my other works there, and maybe a free short story or two. Feel free to send me an email at ballagh-writes@gmail.com, or follow me on Twitter @JonathanBallagh. I'd love to hear what you think.

A parting thought. If you enjoyed the story, I hope you'll help me spread the word. One way you can do so is by leaving a review, even if it's just a few words. Reviews are absolutely critical to the successes of indie authors, and I would be grateful if you'd consider leaving one. Your support means the world.

Thank you.

Jonathan Ballagh